Praise for
A CHRISTMAS JOURNEY

"That rarest of seasonal thrillers: one that exemplifies the message and spirit of the holiday . . . has an almost Jamesian subtlety, and with its powerful message of responsibility and redemption—'We need both to forgive and to be forgiven'—it conveys a moral force in keeping with the season."
—*The Wall Street Journal*

"A doozy of a Christmas mystery."
—*The Dallas Morning News*

"This Victorian-era Christmas offering will surprise and delight."
—*Bookpage*

Praise for
A CHRISTMAS VISITOR

"Satisfyingly dark and suspenseful."
—*Entertainment Weekly*

"Another heartfelt but controlled tale in which an oblique spiritual light seems to glisten on temporal surfaces."
—*The Wall Street Journal*

"Perry . . . owns the Victorian era with her excellent mysteries."
—Minneapolis *Star Tribune*

By Anne Perry
(published by The Random House Publishing Group)

Featuring William Monk
THE FACE OF A STRANGER
A DANGEROUS MOURNING
DEFEND AND BETRAY
A SUDDEN, FEARFUL DEATH
THE SINS OF THE WOLF
CAIN HIS BROTHER
WEIGHED IN THE BALANCE
THE SILENT CRY
A BREACH OF PROMISE
THE TWISTED ROOT
SLAVES OF OBSESSION
FUNERAL IN BLUE
DEATH OF A STRANGER
THE SHIFTING TIDE
DARK ASSASSIN

Featuring Charlotte and Thomas Pitt
THE CATER STREET HANGMAN
CALLANDER SQUARE
PARAGON WALK
RESURRECTION ROW
BLUEGATE FIELDS
RUTLAND PLACE
DEATH IN THE DEVIL'S ACRE
CARDINGTON CRESCENT
SILENCE IN HANOVER CLOSE

BETHLEHEM ROAD
HIGHGATE RISE
BELGRAVE SQUARE
FARRIERS' LANE
THE HYDE PARK HEADSMAN
TRAITORS GATE
PENTECOST ALLEY
ASHWORTH HALL
BRUNSWICK GARDENS
BEDFORD SQUARE
HALF MOON STREET
THE WHITECHAPEL CONSPIRACY
SOUTHAMPTON ROW
SEVEN DIALS
LONG SPOON LANE

The World War I Novels
NO GRAVES AS YET
SHOULDER THE SKY
ANGELS IN THE GLOOM

The Christmas Novels
A CHRISTMAS JOURNEY
A CHRISTMAS VISITOR
A CHRISTMAS GUEST
A CHRISTMAS SECRET

An ANNE PERRY CHRISTMAS

A CHRISTMAS JOURNEY

A CHRISTMAS VISITOR

Two Holiday Novels

ANNE PERRY

BALLANTINE BOOKS • NEW YORK

2006 Ballantine Books Trade Paperback Edition

A Christmas Journey copyright © 2003 by Anne Perry
A Christmas Visitor copyright © 2004 by Anne Perry

Published in the United States by Fawcett Books, an imprint of The Random House Publishing Group, a division of Random House, Inc., New York.

BALLANTINE and colophon are registered trademarks of Random House, Inc.

Originally published in hardcover in the United States as two separate books entitled *A Christmas Journey* and *A Christmas Visitor* by Ballantine Books, an imprint of the Random House Publishing Group, a division of Random House, Inc., in 2003 and 2004.

ISBN 0-345-49700-7

Printed in the United States of America

www.ballantinebooks.com

9 8 7 6 5 4 3 2 1

A CHRISTMAS JOURNEY

To all those who
contribute to the gift of friendship

PART ONE

$\mathcal{L}$ADY VESPASIA CUMMING-GOULD HESITATED A moment at the top of the stairs. Applecross was one of those magnificent country houses where one descended down a long curved sweep of marble into the vast hall where the assembled guests were gathered awaiting the call to dinner.

First one person, then another looked up. To wait for them all would have been ostentatious. She was dressed in oyster satin, not a shade everyone could wear, but Prince Albert himself had said that she was the most beautiful woman in Europe, with her glorious hair and exquisite bones. It was not a remark that had endeared her to the queen, the more so since it was probably true.

But this was not a royal occasion; it was a simple weekend party early in December. The London season was over with its hectic social round, and those who had country homes had returned to them to look

3

forward to Christmas. There were rumors of possible war in the Crimea, but apart from that the middle of the century saw only greater progress and prosperity within an empire that spanned the globe.

Omegus Jones came to the foot of the stairs to meet her. He was not only the perfect host, but also a friend of some years, even though he was in his fifties and Vespasia barely past thirty. Her husband, older than she, was the one who had first made the acquaintance, but he was abroad on business at the moment. Her children were in the house in London, safe and well cared for.

"My dear Vespasia, you are quite ravishing," Omegus said with a self-deprecating smile. "Of which you cannot fail to be aware, so please do not insult my intelligence by pretending surprise, or worse still, denial." He was a lean man with a wry face, full of humor and an unconscious elegance as much at home in a country lane as a London withdrawing room.

She accepted the compliment with a simple "Thank you." A witty reply would have been inappropriate. Besides, Omegus's candor had robbed her of the ability to think of one.

A dozen people were here, including herself. The most socially prominent were Lord and Lady Salchester, closely followed by Sir John and Lady Warburton. Lady Warburton's sister had married a duke, as she found a dozen ways of reminding people. Actually Vespasia's father had been an earl, but she never spoke of it. It was birth, not achievement, and those who mattered already knew. To remind people was indelicate, as if you had no other worth to yourself, never mind to them.

Also present were Fenton and Blanche Twyford; two eminently eligible young men, Peter Hanning and Bertie Rosythe; Gwendolen Kilmuir, widowed more than a year ago; and Isobel Alvie, whose husband had died nearly three years earlier.

It was not customary to serve refreshments before dinner, but rather simply to converse until the butler should sound the gong. The guests would then go into the dining room in strict order of precedence, the rules for which were set out in the finest detail and must never be broken.

Lady Salchester, a formidable horsewoman, was dressed in a deep wine shade, with a crinoline skirt of daunting proportions. She was speaking of last season's races, in particular the meeting at Royal Ascot.

"Magnificent creature!" she said enthusiastically, her voice booming a little. "Nothing else stood a chance."

Lady Warburton smiled as if in agreement.

Bertie Rosythe—slender, fair, superbly tailored—was trying to mask his boredom, and doing it rather well. If Vespasia had not known him, she might have been duped into imagining he was interested in horse-flesh.

Isobel was beside her, darkly striking, less than beautiful but with fine eyes and a ready wit.

"Magnificent creature indeed," she whispered. "And Lady Salchester herself certainly never had a chance."

"What are you talking about?" Vespasia asked, knowing that there must be many layers to the remark.

"Fanny Oakley," Isobel replied, leaning even more closely. "Didn't you see her at Ascot? Whatever were you doing?"

"Watching the horses," Vespasia answered dryly.

"Don't be absurd!" Isobel laughed. "Good heavens! You didn't have money on them, did you? I mean real money?"

Vespasia saw by Isobel's face that she was suddenly concerned in case Vespasia were in gambling debt, not an unheard-of difficulty for a young woman of considerable means and very little to occupy herself, her husband away a good deal of the time, and endless staff to care for her home and her children.

Vespasia wondered for a chill moment if Isobel were really acute enough in her observation to have seen the vague, sad stirrings of emptiness in Vespasia's marriage, and to have at least half understood them. One wished to have friends—without them life would hold only shallow pleasures—but there were areas of the heart into which one did not intrude. Some aches could be borne only in secret. Isobel could not have guessed what had happened in Rome during the passionate revolutions of 1848. No one could. That was a once-in-a-lifetime love, to be buried now and thought of only in dreams. Vespasia would not meet Mario Corena again. This here in Applecross was the world of reality.

"Not at all," she replied lightly. "The race does not need the edge of money to make it fun."

"Are you referring to the horses?" Isobel asked softly.

"Was there another?" Vespasia retorted.

Isobel laughed.

Lord Salchester saw Vespasia and acknowledged her appreciatively. Lady Salchester smiled with warm lips and a glacial eye. "Good evening, Lady Vespasia," she said with penetrating clarity. "How charming to see you. You seem quite recovered from the exertion of the season." It was a less-than-kind reference to a summer cold that had made Vespasia tired and far from herself at the Henley Regatta. "Let us hope next year is not too strenuous for you," she added. She was twenty years older than Vespasia, but a woman of immense stamina who had never been beautiful.

Vespasia was aware of Lord Salchester's eye on her, and even more of Omegus Jones's. It was the latter that tempered her reply. Wit was not always funny, if it cut those already wounded. "I hope so," she answered. "It is tedious for everybody when someone cannot keep up. I shall endeavor not to do that again."

Isobel was surprised. Lady Salchester was astounded.

Vespasia smiled sweetly and excused herself.

Gwendolen Kilmuir was talking earnestly to Bertie Rosythe. Her head was bent a trifle, the light shining on her rich brown hair and the deep plum pink of her gown. She was widowed well over a year now, and had only recently taken the opportunity to cast aside her black. She was a young woman, barely twenty-eight, and had no intention of spending longer in mourning than society demanded. She looked up demurely at Bertie, but she was smiling, and her face had a softness and a warmth to it that was hard to mistake.

Vespasia glanced at Isobel and caught a pensive look in her eye. Then a moment later she smiled, and it was gone.

Bertie turned and saw them. As always he was gracefully polite. Gwendolen's pleasure was not as easily assumed. Vespasia saw the muscles in her neck and chin tighten and her bosom swell as she breathed deeply before mustering a smile. "Good evening, Lady Vespasia, Mrs. Alvie. How nice it will be to dine together."

"As always," Isobel murmured. "I believe we dined at Lady Cranbourne's also, during the summer? And at the queen's garden party." Her eyes flickered up and down Gwendolen's plum taffeta. "I remember your gown."

Gwendolen blushed. Bertie smiled uncertainly.

Suddenly and with a considerable jolt, Vespasia realized that Isobel's interest in Bertie was not as casual as she had supposed. The barb in her remark betrayed her. Such cruelty was not in the character she knew.

"You remember her gown?" she said in feigned surprise. "How delightful." She looked with slight disdain at Isobel's russet gold with its sweeping skirts. "So few gowns are remarkable these days, don't you think?"

Isobel caught her breath, a flare of temper in her eyes.

Gwendolen laughed with a release of tension and turned to Bertie again.

Lady Warburton joined them, and the conversation became enmeshed in gossip, cases of "he said" and "she said" and "do you really believe?"

Dinner was announced, and Omegus Jones offered his arm to Vespasia, which in view of Lady Salchester's presence she found a singular honor, and they went into the long blue-and-gold dining room in solemn and correct procession, each to their appointed place at the glittering table.

The chandeliers above were reflected in the gleam of silver, shattered prisms of light on tiers of crystal goblets in a field of linen napkins folded like lilies.

The fire burned warm in the grate. White chrysanthemums from the greenhouse filled the bowls, providing a redolence of earth and autumn leaves, the soft fragrance of woodland.

They began with the lightest consommé. There would be nine courses, but it was not expected that everyone would eat from all of them. Ladies in particular, mindful of the delicate figures and tiny waists demanded by fashion, would choose with care. Where physical survival was relatively easy, one created rules to make social survival more difficult. Not to be accepted was to become an outcast, a person who fitted nowhere.

Conversation turned to more serious topics. Sir John Warburton spoke of the current political situation, giving his views with gravity, his thin hands brown against the white linen of the cloth.

"Do you really think it will come to war?" Peter Hanning asked with a frown.

"With Russia?" Sir John raised his eyebrows. "It is not impossible."

"Nonsense!" Lord Salchester said briskly, his wineglass in the air. "Nobody's going to go to war against us! Especially over something as absurd as the Crimea! They'll remember Waterloo, and leave us well alone."

"Waterloo was over thirty-five years ago," Omegus Jones pointed out. "The men who fought that have laid their swords by long ago."

"The British army is still the same, sir!" Salchester retorted, his mustache bristling.

"Indeed, I fear it is," Omegus agreed quietly, his lips tight, his eyes sad and far away.

"That was the finest, most invincible army in the world." Salchester's voice grew louder.

"We beat Napoleon," Omegus corrected. "We have fought no one since then. Times change. Good and evil do not, nor pride and compassion, but warfare moves all the time—new weapons, new ideas, new strategies."

"I do not like to disagree with you at your own table, sir," Salchester responded. "Courtesy prevents me from telling you what I think of your view."

Omegus's face lit with a sudden smile, remarkably sweet and quite unaffected. "Let us hope that nothing happens to prove which one of us is correct."

Footmen in livery and parlor maids with white lace-trimmed aprons removed the soup plates and served the fish. The butler poured wine. The lights blazed. The clink of silver on porcelain was the soft background as conversation began again.

Vespasia watched rather than listened. Faces, gestures told her more of emotion than the carefully considered words. She saw how often Gwendolen looked toward Bertie Rosythe, the flush in her face, how easily she laughed when he was amusing, and that it pleased him. He was almost as much aware of her, although he was more careful not to show it quite so openly.

Vespasia was not the only person to notice. She saw Blanche Twyford's satisfaction and recalled hearing her make a remark, which now she understood more clearly. Blanche had spoken of spring weddings, and Gwendolen had blushed. Perhaps this was the weekend when a declaration was expected? It would seem so.

Fenton Twyford seemed less pleased. His dark face looked cautious. A couple of times his glance at Bertie suggested unease, as if an old shadow crossed his thoughts, but Vespasia had no idea what it might be. Was Bertie not quite as perfectly eligible as he seemed? Or was it Gwendolen who somehow fell short? As far as Vespasia knew, she was of good family, wealthy if undistinguished, and without a breath of scandal attached. Her late husband, Roger Kilmuir, was also without blemish and was connected to the aristocracy. If his far elder brother died childless, which seemed likely, then Roger would have inherited the title and all that went with it.

Only, Roger had died in an unfortunate accident, the sort of thing that happened now and again to even the best horsemen. Gwendolen had been quite shattered at the time. It was good to see that she was reaching after some kind of happiness again.

One by one gold-rimmed plates were removed, fresh courses brought, and more wine poured, until nothing was left but mounds of fresh grapes from the hothouse, and silver finger bowls to remove any faint traces of stickiness.

The ladies excused themselves to the withdrawing room and left the gentlemen to pass the port and, for those who so wished, to smoke.

Vespasia followed Isobel and Lady Salchester and was aware of the rustle of taffetas and silks as Gwendolen and Blanche Twyford came behind them. They took their seats in the velvet-curtained withdrawing room, carefully arranging mountainous skirts both to be flattering and not to impede other people's approach, when the gentlemen should rejoin them.

This was the part of any evening that Vespasia liked the least. Conversation almost always became domestic, and since Rome she found it hard to concentrate on such things. She loved her children, deeply and instinctively, and her marriage was agreeable enough. Her husband was kind and intelligent—an honorable man. Many women would have been envious of so much. She wanted for nothing socially or materially. It was only in the longing of the heart, the hunger to care to the power and depth of her being, that she was not answered.

She looked at the other women in the room and wondered what lay behind the gracious masks of their faces. Lady Salchester had energy and intelligence, but she was plain, plainer than her own parlor maid, and probably the housemaid and the kitchen maid, as well. It was widely suspected that Lord Salchester's attention wandered, in a practical as well as imaginary way.

"I know what you are thinking," Isobel said beside her, leaning a little closer so she could speak in a whisper.

Vespasia was startled. "Do you?"

"Of course!" Isobel smiled. "I was thinking so, too. And it is quite unfair. If she were to do the same, with that nice-looking footman, society would be scandalized, and she would be ruined. She would never go anywhere again!"

"Dozens of married women become bored with their husbands, and after they have produced the appropriate number of children, they have affairs," Vespasia pointed out sadly. "I don't think I admire it, but I am quite aware that it occurs. I could name you half a dozen."

"So could I," Isobel agreed flippantly. "We'll have to do it, and see if we know the same ones."

Blanche Twyford was talking to Gwendolen, nodding every now and then, and Gwendolen was smiling. It was easy to guess the subject of their excitement.

Vespasia looked sideways at Isobel and saw the shadow in her eyes again. If Bertie proposed marriage to Gwendolen this weekend, which seemed to be generally expected, would Isobel really lose more than a possible admirer? Did she care for him, perhaps even have hopes herself? She had loved her husband; Vespasia knew that. But he had been gone for three years now, and Isobel was a young woman, no more than Vespasia's own age. It was possible to fall in love again. In fact, at thirty it would be harsh and lonely not to.

Should she say something? Was this a time when real friendship dared embarrassment and rejection? Or was silence, the pretense of not knowing, preferable, thereby allowing the deeper wounds to remain private?

The decision was taken from her by the arrival of Lady Warburton, whereupon the conversation moved to fashion, Prince Albert's latest ideas for improving the mind, and, of course, the queen's enthusiasm for everything her husband said.

They were rejoined by the gentlemen, and the atmosphere changed again. Everyone became more self-conscious, backs a little straighter, laughter more delicate, movement more graceful. The servants had retreated to leave them alone. The final cleaning up would be done when the guests retired to bed.

They were all facing Gwendolen and Bertie when Isobel made the remark. Gwendolen was sitting with her skirts swept around her like a tide, her head up, her slender throat pale in the candlelight. She looked beautiful and triumphant. Bertie stood close to her, just a little possessively.

"Charming," Lady Warburton said very quietly, as if the announcement had already been made.

Vespasia looked at Isobel and saw the strain in her face. She felt a moment's deep sorrow for her. Whatever the prize, defeat is a bitter taste.

Peter Hanning was saying something trivial, and everyone laughed. There was a goblet of water on the side table. Gwendolen asked for it.

Bertie reached across swiftly and picked it up, then set it on the tray, which had been left there. He passed it to her, balanced in one hand, bowing as he did so. "Madame," he said humbly. "Your servant forever."

Gwendolen put out her hand.

"For heaven's sake, you look like a footman!" Isobel's voice was clear and brittle. "Surely you aspire to be more than that? She's hardly going to give her favors to a servant! At least, not permanently!"

The moment froze. It was a dreadful statement, and Vespasia winced.

"She will require a gentleman," Isobel went on. "After all, Kilmuir could look forward to a title." She turned to Gwendolen. "Couldn't he?"

Gwendolen was white. "I love the man," she said huskily. "The status means nothing to me."

Isobel raised her eyebrows very high. "You would give yourself to him if he were really a footman?" she asked incredulously. "My dear, I believe you!"

Gwendolen stared at her, but her gaze was inward, as if she saw a horror beyond description, almost beyond endurance. Then slowly she rose to her feet, her eyes hollow. She seemed a trifle unsteady.

"Gwendolen!" Bertie said quickly, but she walked past him as if suddenly he were invisible to her. She stumbled to the door, needing a moment or two to grasp the handle and turn it, then went out into the hall.

Lady Warburton turned on Isobel. "Really, Mrs. Alvie, I know you imagine that you are amusing, at least at times, but that remark merely exposed your envy, and it is most unbecoming." She swiveled to face Omegus Jones. "If you will excuse me, I shall make sure that poor Gwendolen is all right." And with a crackle of skirts she swept out.

There was an uncomfortable silence. Vespasia decided to take control before the situation degenerated. She turned to Isobel. "I don't think this can be salvaged with any grace. We would do better to retreat and leave well enough alone. Come. It is late anyway."

Isobel hesitated only a moment, glancing at the ring of startled and embarrassed faces, and realized she could only agree.

Outside in the hall Vespasia took her arm, forcing her to stop before she reached the bottom of the stairs. "What on earth has got hold of you?" she demanded. "You will have to apologize to Gwendolen tomorrow, and to everyone else. Being in love with Bertie does not excuse what you did, and you would be a great deal better off if you had not made yourself so obvious!"

Isobel glared at her, her face ashen but for the high spots of color in her cheeks, but she was too close to tears to answer. She was now perfectly aware of how foolish she had been, and that she had made not Gwendolen but herself look vulnerable. She shook her arm free and stormed up the stairs without looking backwards.

Vespasia did not sleep well. Certainly Isobel had behaved most unfortunately, but marriage, with love or without it, was a very serious business. For a woman it was the only honorable occupation, and battles for an eligible man of the charm and the financial means of someone like Bertie Rosythe were fought to the last ditch. She hurt for the pain Isobel must feel, a pain she had just made a great deal worse for herself. Vespasia could only imagine it. Her own marriage had been easily arranged. Her father was an earl, and she herself was startlingly beautiful. She could have been a duchess had she wished. She preferred a man of intelligence and an ambition to do something useful, and who loved her for herself and gave her a great deal of freedom. It was a good bargain. The kind of love for which she hungered was well lost and offered to very few—and belonged in dreams and hot Roman summers of manning the barricades against overwhelming odds. One loves utterly, and then yields to honor and duty and returns home to live with other realities, leaving the height and the ache of passion behind.

She rose in the morning and, with her maid's assistance of course, dressed warmly in a blue-gray woolen gown against the December frost and a very sharp wind whining in the eaves and seeking to find every crack in the windows. She went downstairs to face the other guests and whatever difficulties the night had not resolved.

She was met in the hall by Omegus Jones. He was wearing an outdoor jacket and there was mud on his boots. His dark hair was untidy, and his face was so pale he looked waxen.

"Vespasia . . ."

"Whatever is it?" She went to him immediately. "You look ill! Can I help?" She touched his hand lightly. It was freezing—and wet. Suddenly she was frightened. Omegus, more than anyone else she knew, always seemed in control of himself, and of events. "What is it?" she said again, more urgently.

He did not prevaricate. He closed his icy hand over hers with great gentleness. "I am afraid we have just found Gwendolen's body in the lake." He gestured vaguely behind him to the sheet of ornamental water beyond the sloping lawn with its cedars and herbaceous border. "We have brought her out, but there is nothing to be done for her. She seems to have been dead since sometime last night."

Vespasia was stunned. It was impossible. "How can she have fallen in?" she said, denying the thought desperately. "It is shallow at the edges. There are flowers growing there, reeds! You would simply get stuck in the mud! And anyway, why on earth would she go walking down by the water on a December night? Why would anyone?"

He looked haggard, and he was unmoved by her arguments, except to pity.

Vespasia was touched by a deep fear.

"I'm sorry, my dear," he answered, his eyes hollow. "She went in from the bridge, where it is quite deep. The only conclusion possible seems to be that she jumped, of her own accord. The balustrade is quite high enough to prevent an accidental falling, even in the dark. I had them made that way myself."

"Omegus! I'm so sorry!" Her first thought was for him, and the distress it would cause him, the dark shadow over the beauty of Applecross. It was a loveliness more than simply that of a great house where art and nature had combined to create a perfect landscape of flowers, trees, water, and views to the hills and fields beyond. It was a place of peace where generations of love of the land had sunk into its fabric and left a residue of warmth, even in the starkness of late autumn.

Approached from the southwest along an avenue

of towering elms, the classic Georgian facade looked toward the afternoon sun over the downs. The gravel forecourt was fronted by a balustrade with a long, shallow flight of stone steps that led down to the vast lawn, beyond which lay the ornamental water.

"I'm afraid it will become most unpleasant," he said unhappily. "People will be frightened because sudden death of the young is a terrible reminder of the fragility of all life. She had seemed on the brink of new joy after her bereavement, and it has been snatched away from her. Only the boldest of us, and the least imaginative, do not sometimes in the small hours of the morning also fear the same for ourselves. And they will not understand why it has happened. They will look for someone to blame, because anger is easier to live with than fear."

"I don't understand!" she said with a gulp. "Why on earth would she do such a thing? Isobel was cruel, but if anyone should be mortified, it is she! She betrayed her own vulnerability in front of those who will have no understanding and little mercy."

"We know that, my dear Vespasia, but they do not," he said softly, still touching her so lightly she felt only the coldness of his fingers. "They will see only a woman with every cause to expect an offer of marriage, but who was publicly insulted by suggestions that she is a seeker after position rather than a woman in love." His face twisted with irony. "Which is an absurd piece of hypocrisy, I am aware. We have created a society in which it is necessary for a woman to marry well if she is to succeed, because we have contrived for it to be impossible for her to achieve any safety or success alone, even should she wish to. But frequently we criticize most vehemently that which is largely our own doing."

"Are you . . . are you saying that Isobel's remark drove her to commit suicide?" Vespasia's voice cracked as if her mouth and throat were parched.

"It seems so," he admitted. "Unless there was an exchange between Bertie and Gwendolen after she left the withdrawing room, and a quarrel she did not feel she could repair."

Vespasia could think of nothing to say. It was hideous.

"You offered to help me," Omegus reminded her. "I may ask that you do."

"How?"

"I have very little idea," he confessed. "Perhaps that is why I need you."

Vespasia swallowed hard. "I shall tell Isobel," she said, wondering how on earth she could make such a thing bearable. The day yawned ahead like an abyss, full of grief and confusion.

"Thank you," he accepted. "I shall have the servants ask everyone to be at breakfast, and tell them then."

She nodded, then turned and went back upstairs and along to Isobel's room. She knocked on the door and waited until she heard Isobel's voice tell her to go in.

Isobel was lying in the bed, her dark hair spread across the pillow, her eyes shadowed around as if she, too, had slept badly. She sat up slowly, staring at Vespasia in surprise.

There was no mercy in hesitation. Vespasia sat on the bed facing Isobel. "I have just met Omegus in the hall," she began. "They have found Gwendolen's body in the lake. The only conclusion possible from the circumstances is that sometime after our unfortunate conversation in the withdrawing room she must have gone out alone and, in some derangement of mind, jumped off the bridge. I'm afraid it is very bad."

Isobel sat up, pulling the sheet around herself, even though the room was not cold. "Is she . . . ?"

"Of course. It is December! If she had not drowned, she would have frozen."

"But surely she must have fallen!" Isobel protested, pushing her hair off her face. "Why on earth would she jump? That's ridiculous!" She shook her head. "It can't be true!"

"If you remember, the balustrade along the bridge is too high to fall over by accident," Vespasia reminded her. "Anyway, why on earth would she be out there leaning over the bridge at eleven o'clock on a December night? And alone!"

The little color in Isobel's face had drained away, leaving her pasty-white. She started to shiver. Her hands were clenched in the sheets.

"Are you implying that my idiotic remark made her do that? Why? All I did was insult her! She wouldn't be the first woman to be called greedy, or desperate. That's absurd!" Her voice was sharp, a little high-pitched.

"Isobel, there is no point in pretending that it did not happen," Vespasia said steadily, trying to sound reasonable, although she did not feel it. "You are going to have to go down at some time and face everyone, whatever they believe. And the longer you delay it, the more you will appear to be accepting the blame."

"I'm not to blame!" Isobel said indignantly. "I was rash in what I said, and I would have apologized to her today. But if she went and jumped off the bridge, that has nothing to do with me, and I won't have anyone say that it has!" She flung the sheets aside and climbed out of the bed, stumbling a little as she stood up. She kept her back to Vespasia, as though blaming her for having brought the news. But Vespasia noticed that when Isobel picked up her peignoir, her fingers were stiff, and when it slipped out of her grasp, it took her three attempts to retrieve it.

24

*B*reakfast was ghastly. When Vespasia and Isobel arrived, everyone else was already gathered around the table. Food was laid out on the sideboard in silver chafing dishes: finnan haddock, kedgeree, eggs, sausage, deviled kidneys, and bacon. There was also plenty of fresh crisp toast, butter, marmalade, and tea. People had served themselves, as a matter of good manners, before Omegus Jones had divulged what had occurred, but nobody felt like eating.

Isobel's entrance had been greeted in silence, nor did anyone meet her eyes.

Vespasia looked at Omegus and saw the warning and the apology unspoken in his expression.

Isobel hesitated. No one was wearing black, because no one had foreseen the occasion, and of course Isobel was the only one who had known of the death before dressing. She wore a sober dark green.

Lady Warburton was the first to acknowledge her presence, but it was with a chilly stare, her rather ordinary face pinched with distaste. She regarded Isobel's clothes first, long before her face. "I see you were aware of the tragedy before you dressed," she said coolly. "In fact, perhaps last night?"

"My dear Evelyn, do not let your grief . . . ," Sir John began, then trailed away as his wife turned to glare at him.

"It is perfectly obvious she was aware of poor

Gwendolen's death!" she said in a low, grating voice. "Why else would she wear mourning to breakfast?"

"Hypocrite," Blanche Twyford murmured half under her breath. No one doubted that she was referring to Isobel, not Lady Warburton.

Isobel pretended not to have heard. She took a slice of toast, and then found herself unable to swallow it. She played with it to keep her hands occupied, and perhaps to prevent anyone else from noticing that they trembled.

Bertie looked haggard and utterly confused.

Vespasia wondered if he had gone after Gwendolen last night. Surely he must have. Or was it conceivable he had not? If he had followed her and told her of his feelings, asked her to marry him as everyone was expecting, nothing Isobel Alvie, or anyone else, could have said would have destroyed her happiness. Was that what he was thinking, that he avoided her eyes now? And what about Lady Warburton? Had she followed Gwendolen, or merely said she would to escape the situation?

"This is perfectly dreadful!" Lady Salchester burst out. "We really cannot sit here not knowing what has happened, and having no idea what to say to each other!"

"We know what has happened," Blanche Twyford said angrily. "Mrs. Alvie spoke inexcusably last night, and poor Mrs. Kilmuir was so distraught that she took her own life. It's as plain as the nose on your face."

Lady Salchester froze. "I beg your pardon?" she said, ice dripping from her voice.

"For heaven's sake!" Blanche flushed. "I did not mean it personally. It is an expression of—of clarity. We all know perfectly well what happened!"

"I don't." Lord Salchester came surprisingly to his wife's aid. "To me it is as much of a muddle as the nose on your face!"

Vespasia wanted to laugh hysterically. She suppressed the desire with difficulty, holding her napkin to her lips and pretending to sneeze.

Blanche Twyford glared at Lord Salchester.

Salchester opened his blue eyes very wide. "Why on earth should a perfectly healthy young woman on the brink of matrimony throw herself into the lake? Merely because her rival insults her? I don't understand." He looked baffled. He shook his head. "Women," he said unhappily. "If she had been a chap, she'd simply have insulted her back, and they'd have gone to bed friends."

"Oh, do be quiet, Ernest!" Lady Salchester snapped at him. "You are talking complete nonsense!"

"Am I?" he said mildly. "Wasn't she going to be married? That's what everyone said!"

Bertie stood up, white-faced, and left the room.

"Good God! He's not going to the lake, is he?" Salchester asked, his napkin sliding to the floor.

Isobel left the table, as well, only she went out the other door, toward the garden, even though it was raining and not much above freezing outside.

"Guilt!" Lady Warburton said viciously.

"I think that's a little harsh," Sir John expostulated. "She was—"

"Both of them!" his wife cut across, effectively cutting off whatever he had been going to say. He lapsed into silence.

Omegus rose to his feet. "Lady Vespasia, I wonder if I might talk with you in the library?"

"Of course." She was grateful for the chance to escape the ghastly meal table. She scraped her chair back before the footman could pull it out for her.

"You're not going to just leave it!" Lady Warburton accused him. "This cannot be run away from. I won't allow it!"

Omegus looked at her coldly. "I am going to think before I act, Lady Warburton. An error now, even if made with the purest of motives, could cause grief which could not later be undone. Excuse me." And leaving her angry, and now confounded, he left the room with Vespasia at his heels.

In the silence of the book-lined library with its exquisite bronzes he closed the door and turned to face her. "Evelyn Warburton is right," he said grimly. There was intense sadness in his eyes, and the lines around his mouth were drawn down.

"It was foolish," she agreed. "And unkind. Both

are faults, but not in any way crimes, or most of society would be in prison. It is dreadful that Gwendolen should have taken her life, but surely it is because she believed that Bertie would not marry her after all? It cannot be simply that Isobel behaved so badly."

He regarded her with patience. "It is not necessarily what is but what is perceived that society will judge," he answered. "Whether it is fair or not will enter into it very little. If we allow it to pass without addressing it, each time it is retold it will grow worse. What Isobel actually said will be lost in the exaggerations until no one remembers the truth. Tales alter every time they are retold, and, my dear, you must know that." There was a faint reproof in his voice.

Of course she knew it, and felt the color burn in her face for her evasion. "What can we do?" she said helplessly. "What do you suppose the truth is? And how will we ever know? Gwendolen can't tell us, and if Bertie quarreled with her, do you imagine he will tell us, in view of what has happened? Did Lady Warburton go after her? Do you know?"

"Apparently not. Do you know anything of medieval trials when someone was accused of a crime?" he asked.

She was astounded. Surely he could not have said what she thought she had heard. "I beg your pardon?"

Somewhere in the garden a dog was barking, and a servant's rapid footsteps crossed the hall. The ghost of a smile curved his lips. "I am not referring to trial by combat, or by ordeal. I was thinking of a process of discovering the truth so far as we are able. If Isobel is indeed guilty of anything, or if Bertie is, then all of us agreeing upon a form of expiation would absolve them of guilt, after which we would make a solemn covenant that the matter would be considered closed."

A wild hope flared up inside her. "But would we?" she said, struggling to believe it. "Would we agree to it? And could we find the truth? What if the guilty person would not accept the expiation?" She lifted her shoulders very slightly. "And what could it be? What if they simply walk away? We have no power to enforce anything. Why should they trust us to keep silent afterwards, let alone to forgive?"

He walked over to the heavy velvet curtains and the window overlooking the parkland with its rolling grass and great trees, now winter bare. Rain spattered against the glass.

"I have thought about it," he said, as much to himself as to her. "The idea always appealed to me, the belief in expiation and forgiveness, a new start. Surely that is the only hope for any of us. We need both to forgive and to be forgiven."

Looking at him standing with the harsh light on his face, she saw more pain inside him than she had in the years she had known him, and also a far greater understanding of peace. In that instant she wished above all to fulfill this faith in her, to make him pleased that it was she to whom he had turned.

"But why should they agree?" she said anxiously. "We have no power other than persuasion."

He smiled and turned to face her. "Oh, but we have! The power of society is almost infinite, my dear. To be excluded is a kind of death. And if one is spoken of with sufficient venom, invitations cease, doors are closed, and one becomes invisible. People pass one by without a glance. One finds that in all ways that matter, one no longer exists. A young woman becomes unmarriageable. A young man has no career, no position; all clubs are closed to him."

It was true. Vespasia had seen it. It was the cruelest fate because the people to whom it could happen were unfitted for any other life. They did not know how to earn a living in the work done by ordinary men and women. Those occupations also were closed to them. No woman born a lady could suddenly become a maid or a laundress. Even had she the skills, the temperament, and the stamina, she was not acceptable either to an employer of the class she used to be, or to the other employees to whose class she did not belong, nor ever could.

And she was not fitted or trained for any of the other occupations in which a woman could earn her way.

Suddenly Vespasia realized just what might be ahead

for Isobel, and she felt cold and sick. "How will that help us?" she said huskily.

He looked at her with great earnestness. "If I explain to everyone what I have in mind, and they agree, then they will all be bound by it," he answered. "The punishment for breaking their word would be exactly that same ostracism which will be applied to whoever is found at fault in Gwendolen's death. Anyone who refuses to abide by that brands himself as outside the group of the rest of us. No one will wish to do that." He shook his head a tiny fraction, lips tight. "Don't tell me it is coercion. I know. Few people accept the judgment of their peers without it. It will offer a way for us to prevent the pain, and perhaps injustice, that may result otherwise." His voice became softer. "And as important, it will at least give Isobel, or Bertie if it is he to blame, a chance to expiate the act of cruelty they may have performed."

"How?" she asked.

"Gwendolen left a letter behind," he explained. "It is sealed, and will remain so. It is addressed to her mother, Mrs. Naylor, who lives near Inverness, in the far north of Scotland. We could post it, but that would be a harsh way for a mother to find out that her child has destroyed the life she labored to give."

Vespasia was appalled. "You mean they would have to go to this unhappy woman and give her the letter? That's . . ." She was lost for words. Isobel would never do it! Neither would Bertie Rosythe. They would neither of them have the heart, or the stomach, for it. Not to mention making the journey to the north of Scotland in December.

Omegus raised his eyebrows. "Do you expect to be forgiven without pain, without a pilgrimage that costs the mind, the body, and the heart?"

"I don't think it will work."

"Will you at least help me try?"

She looked at him standing, lean, oddly graceful, the lines deeper in his face in the morning light, and she could not refuse. "Of course."

"Thank you," he said solemnly.

*W*hat?" Lord Salchester said with stinging disbelief when they were gathered together at the luncheon table. The first course was finished when Omegus requested their attention and began to explain to them his plan.

"Preposterous!" Lady Warburton agreed. "We all know perfectly well what happened. For heaven's sake, we saw it!"

"Heard it," Sir John corrected.

She glared at him.

"Actually," he went on. "It's not a bad idea at all."

Lady Warburton swung around in her chair and fixed him with a glacial eye. "It is ridiculous. And if we find Mrs. Alvie guilty, as we will do, what difference will that make?"

"That is not the end of the issue," Omegus exclaimed. Vespasia saw him struggling to keep the dislike from his face. "In medieval times not all crimes were punished by execution or imprisonment," he went on. "Sometimes the offender was permitted to make a pilgrimage of expiation. If he returned, which in those dangerous times very often he did not, then the sin was considered to have been washed out. All men were bound to pardon it and take the person back among them as if it had not occurred. It was never spoken of again, and he was trusted and loved as before."

"A pilgrimage?" Peter Hanning said with disbelief, derision close to laughter in his voice. "To where, for heaven's sake? Walsingham? Canterbury? Jerusalem, perhaps? Anyway, travel is a relative pleasure these days, if one can afford it. I'm not a religious man. I don't care a fig if Mrs. Alvie, or anyone else, makes a journey to some holy place."

"You have missed the point, Peter," Omegus told him. "I shall choose the journey, and it will not be a pleasure. Nor will it be particularly expensive. But it will be extremely difficult, particularly so for anyone who bears guilt at all for the death of Gwendolen Kil-

34

muir. And if we profess any claim to justice whatsoever, we will not decide in advance who that is."

"I agree," Sir John said immediately.

"So do I," Vespasia added. "I agree to both justice and forgiveness."

"And if I don't?" Lady Warburton asked sharply, looking across at Vespasia, her brow creased with dislike, her mouth pinched.

Vespasia smiled. "Then one would be compelled to wonder why not," she replied.

"I agree," Blanche Twyford said. "Then it need never be spoken of beyond these walls. It will stop gossip among others who were not here, and any slander they may make against any of us, letting their imaginations build all manner of speculation. If we are all bound by what we agree, and the punishment is carried out here, the matter is ours. Surely you agree, don't you?"

"I suppose, if you put it that way," Lady Warburton said reluctantly.

Lord Salchester agreed also.

Omegus looked at Bertie, the question in his face.

"Who is to be the judge of this?" Bertie asked dubiously. Today his elegance seemed haggard, his exquisite suit and cravat an irrelevance.

"Omegus," Vespasia said before anyone else could speak. "He is not involved and we may trust him to be fair."

"May we?" Bertie said. "Applecross is his house. He is most certainly involved."

"He is not involved in Gwendolen's death." Vespasia kept her temper with increasing difficulty. "Do you have someone in mind you prefer?"

"I think the whole idea is absurd," he replied. "And totally impractical."

"I disagree." Lord Salchester spoke with sudden decisiveness, his voice sharp. "I think it is an excellent idea. I am quite happy to be bound by it. So is my wife." He did not consult her. "It will be for the good of all our reputations, and will allow the matter to be dealt with immediately, and justice be served." He looked a little balefully around the table at the others. "Who is against it? Apart from those either guilty or too shortsighted to see the ultimate good."

Omegus smiled bleakly, but he did not point out the loaded nature of the challenge. One by one they all agreed, except Isobel.

Vespasia looked at her very steadily. "Any alternative would be much worse, I believe," she said softly. "Do we all give our word, on pain of being ostracized ourselves should we break it, that we will keep silent, absolutely, on the subject after the judgment is given and should the price be paid? Then the offender, if there is one, begins anew from the day of their return, and we forget the offense as if it had not happened?"

One by one, reluctantly at first, they each gave their pledge.

"Thank you," Omegus said gravely. "Then after luncheon we shall begin."

*T*hey collected in the withdrawing room, the curtains open on the formal garden sweeping down toward the wind-ruffled water of the lake, and the trees beyond. It was the place where they could all be seated in something close to a circle, and the servants were dismissed until they should be called for. No one was to interrupt.

Omegus called them to order, then asked each of them in turn to tell what they knew of Gwendolen Kilmuir's actions, her feelings, and what she may have said to them of her hopes from the time she had arrived three days before.

They began tentatively, unsure how far to trust, but gradually emotions were stirred by memory.

"She was full of hope," Blanche said a little tearfully. "She believed that her time of loss was coming to an end." She shot a look of intense dislike at Isobel. "Kilmuir's death was a terrible blow to her."

"So much so that she intended to marry less than a year and a half later," Peter Hanning observed, leaning back in his chair, his cravat a little crooked, a slight curl to his lip.

"They had had some difficult times," Blanche explained crossly. "He was not an easy man."

"It was she who was not an easy woman," Fenton Twyford interrupted. "She took some time to accept her responsibilities. Kilmuir was very patient with her, but the time came when he bore it less graciously."

"A great deal less graciously," Blanche agreed. "But he was mending his ways. She was looking forward to a far greater warmth between them when he was killed."

"Killed?" Sir John said abruptly.

"In an accident," Blanche told him. "A horse bolted, I believe, and he was thrown out of the trap and dragged. Quite dreadful. When she heard of it, poor Gwendolen was devastated. That was why it was so wonderful that she had a second chance at happiness." She looked at Bertie with intense meaning.

He blushed miserably.

The tale progressed, each person adding colorful details until a picture emerged of the courtship of Bertie and Gwendolen, reaching the point when everyone expected an announcement. More than one person had noticed that Isobel was not pleased, even though she attempted to hide the fact. Now all the thoughts came to the surface, and she was clearly humiliated, but she did not dare escape. It would have been an admission, and she was determined not to make one.

But the tide swept relentlessly on. Even Vespasia was carried along by it until she was placed in a position where she must speak either for Isobel or against her. She had been forced to see more clearly now than at the time how deep the feelings had been on both sides. Under the veneer of wit and a kind of friendship, there had been a struggle for victory, which would have lifted either one woman or the other back onto the crest of a wave in society, assured of comfort and acceptance. The other would be left among the number of women alone, always a little apart, a little lost, hoping for the next invitation, but never certain that it would come, dreading the next bill in case it would not be met.

Without realizing why, Vespasia spoke for Isobel. Gwendolen was beyond her help, and many others were eager to take her part.

"We use what arts we have," she said, looking more at Omegus than the others. "Gwendolen was pretty and charming. She flattered people by allowing them to help her, and she was grateful. Isobel was far too proud for that, and too honest. She used wit, and sometimes it was cruel. I think when Gwendolen was the victim, she affected to be more wounded than she was. She craved sympathy, and she won it. Isobel was foolish enough not to see that."

"If Gwendolen was not really hurt, why did she kill herself?" Blanche demanded angrily, challenge in her eyes and the set of her thin shoulders. "That seems to be taking the cry for sympathy rather too far to be of any use!" Her voice was heavily sarcastic, her smile a sneer.

Vespasia looked at Bertie. "When Gwendolen left last night, after Isobel's remark, did you go after her to see if she was all right?" she asked him. "Did you assure her that you did not for an instant believe she was in love with your money and position rather than with you?"

Bertie colored painfully and his face tightened.

Everyone waited.

"Did you?" Omegus said in a very clear voice.

Bertie looked up. "No. I admit it. Isobel spoke with such . . . certainty, I did wonder. I, God forgive me, I doubted her." He fidgeted. "I started to think of things she had said, things other people had said—warnings." He tried to laugh and failed. "Of course, I realize now that they were merely malicious, born of jealousy. But last night I hesitated. If I hadn't, poor Gwendolen would be alive, and I should not be alone, mourning her loss." The look he gave Isobel was venomous in its intensity and its blame.

Vespasia was stunned. It was the last response she had intended to provoke. Far from helping Isobel, she had sealed her fate.

Omegus also looked wretched, but he was bound by his own rules.

The verdict was a matter of form. By overwhelming majority they found Isobel guilty of unbridled cruelty and deliberate intent to ruin Gwendolen, falsely, in the eyes of the man she loved. There was sympathy for Bertie, but it was not unmixed with a certain contempt.

"And what is this pilgrimage that Mrs. Alvie is to make?" Fenton Twyford asked angrily. "I must say I agree with Peter. I really don't care where she goes, as long as it is not across my path. I can't stand a woman with a vicious tongue. It's inexcusable."

"Very little is inexcusable," Omegus said with sudden cutting authority, his face at once bleak and touched with a terrible compassion. "You have given your word before everyone here that if she completes the journey, you will wipe the matter from your memory as if it did not happen. Otherwise, you will have broken your word—and that also cannot be excused. If a man's oath does not bind him, then he cannot be a part of any civilized society."

Twyford went white. He glanced around the table. No one smiled at him. Lord Salchester nodded in agreement. "Quite so," he said. "Quite so."

"Are we agreed?" Omegus inquired softly.

"We are," came the answer from everyone except Isobel.

Omegus turned to her and waited.

"What journey?" she said huskily.

Omegus explained. "Gwendolen left a letter addressed to her mother, Mrs. Naylor. I have not opened it, nor will you. It's obviously private. You will take it to Mrs. Naylor and explain to her that Gwendolen has taken her own life, and your part in it. If Mrs. Naylor wishes to come to London, or to Applecross, you will accompany her, unless she will not permit you to. But you will do all in your power to succeed. She lives near Inverness, in the Highlands of Scotland. Her address is on the envelope."

The silence in the room was broken by the sound of a sudden shower lashing the windows.

"I won't!" Isobel said in a rush of outrage. "The north of Scotland! At this time of year? And to . . . to face . . . absolutely not." She stood up, her body shaking, her face burning with hectic color. "I will not do it." For a moment she stared at them, and then left the room, grasping the door until it slammed against the farther wall, then swinging it shut after her.

Vespasia half rose also, then realized the futility of it and sat down again.

"I thought she wouldn't," Lady Warburton said with a smile of satisfaction.

Vespasia thought for an instant of a crocodile who fears it is robbed of its prey, and then feels its teeth sink into flesh after all. "You must be pleased," she said aloud. "I imagine you would have found it nigh on impossible to know something unkind about someone and be unable to repeat it to others."

Lady Warburton looked at her coldly, her face suddenly bloodless, eyes glittering. "I would be more careful in my choice of friends, if I were you, Lady Vespasia. Your father's title will not protect you forever. There is a degree of foolishness beyond which even you will have to pay."

"You are suggesting I desert my friends the moment it becomes inconvenient to me?" Vespasia inquired, although there was barely an inflection in her tone, only heavy disgust. "Why does it not astound me that you should say so?" She also rose to her feet. "Excuse me," she said to no one in particular, and left the room.

Outside in the hall she was completely alone. There was no servant in sight, no footman waiting to be called. They had taken Omegus's request for privacy as an absolute order. There was something strangely judicial about it, as if everything, even domestic detail, might be different from now on.

She crossed the wooden parquet and climbed slowly up the great staircase. A few words had changed everything. But they were not merely words: They sprang from thoughts and passions, deep tides that had been there all the time; it was only the knowledge of them that was new.

Vespasia found it difficult to concentrate on dressing for dinner. Her maid suggested one gown after another, but nothing seemed appropriate, nor for once did she really care. The silks, laces, embroidery, the whole palette of subtle and gorgeous colors seemed an empty pleasure. Gwendolen was dead, from whatever despair real or imagined that had gripped her, and Isobel was on the brink of suffering more than she yet understood.

She thought everyone else would be dressing soberly, in grief for Gwendolen, and in parade of their sense of social triumph, somber but victorious. She decided to wear purple. It suited her porcelain skin and the shimmering glory of her hair. It would be beautiful, appropriate for half mourning, and outrageous for a woman of her youth. Altogether it would serve every purpose.

She swept down the stairs again, as she had only an evening ago, to gasps of surprise, and either admiration or envy, depending upon whether it was Lord Salchester or Lady Warburton. The merest glance told her that Isobel was not yet there. Would she have the courage to come?

Omegus was at her elbow, his face carefully smoothed of expression, but she could not mistake the anxiety in his eyes.

"She is not going to run away, is she?" he said so quietly that Blanche Twyford, only a yard or two from them, could not have heard.

Vespasia had exactly the same fear. "I don't know," she admitted. "I think she is very angry. There is a certain injustice in putting the blame entirely upon her. If Bertie was so easily put off, then he did not love Gwendolen with much depth or honor."

"Of course not, my dear," Omegus murmured. "Surely that is the disillusion which really hurt Gwendolen more than she could bear."

Suddenly it made agonizing sense. It was not any suggestion Isobel made. It was the exposing of the shallowness beneath the dreams, the breaking of the thin veneer of hope with which Gwendolen had deceived herself. She had not lost the prize; she had seen that it did not exist, not as she needed it to be.

"Was that really a cruelty?" she said aloud, meeting his eyes for the first time in their whispered conversation.

Omegus did not hesitate. "Yes," he answered. "There are some things to which we need to wake up slowly, and the weaknesses of someone we love are among them."

"But surely she needed to see what a frail creature he is before she married him!" she protested.

He smiled. "Oh, please, think a little longer, a little more deeply, my dear."

She was surprisingly wounded, not bluntly as by a

knife, but deeply and almost without realizing it for the first few seconds, as a razor cuts. She had not been aware until this moment how much she cared what Omegus thought of her.

Perhaps he saw the change in her face. His expression softened.

She found herself pulling away, her pride offended that he should see his power to wound her.

He saw that, too, and he ignored it. "She would have accepted him," he said, still quietly. "She had no better offer, and by the time she had realized his flaws, he might have begun to overcome them, and habit, tenderness, other promises made and kept might have blunted the edge of disappointment, and given other compensations that would have been enough." He put his hand on her arm, so lightly she saw it rather than felt it. "Love is not perfection," he said. "It is tolerance, dreams past, and the future shared. A great deal of it, my dear, is friendship, if it is to last. There is nothing more precious than true friendship. It is the rock upon which all other loves must stand, if they are to endure. She should have made her own decision, not have it made for her by someone else's desperate realization of defeat."

She did not answer. His words filled her mind and left no room for any of her own.

Ten minutes later when Isobel still had not appeared, Vespasia decided to go and fetch her. She went back up the stairs and along the west corridor to

Isobel's room. She knocked and, when there was no answer, turned the handle and went in.

Isobel was standing before the long glass, looking critically at herself. She was not beautiful, but she had a great grace, and in her bronze-and-black gown she looked magnificent, more striking, more dramatic than Gwendolen ever had. Vespasia saw for the first time that that was precisely the trouble. Bertie Rosythe did not want a dramatic wife. He might like to play with fire, but he did not wish to live with it. Isobel could never have won.

"If you do not come now, you are going to be late," Vespasia said calmly.

Isobel swung around, startled. She had obviously been expecting the return of her maid.

"I haven't decided if I am coming yet," she replied. "I didn't hear you knock!"

"I daresay you were too deep in your own thoughts." Vespasia brushed it aside. "You must come," she insisted. "If you don't, you will be seen as having run away, and that would be an admission of guilt."

"They think I am guilty anyway," Isobel said bitterly. "Don't pretend you cannot see that! Even you with so . . ."

Vespasia had been at fault. "I did not intend my remarks to give them that opening," she answered. "I am truly sorry for that. It was far clumsier than I meant it to be."

Isobel kept her head turned away. "I daresay they would have come to the same place anyway, just taken a little longer. But it would have been easier for me had the final blow not come from a friend."

"Then you may consider yourself revenged," Vespasia said. "I am subtly chastened, and guilty of my own sin. Are you now coming down to dinner? The longer you leave it, the more difficult it will be. That is the truth, whoever is to blame for anything."

Isobel turned around very slowly. "Why are you wearing purple, for heaven's sake? Is anyone else in mourning?"

Vespasia smiled bleakly. "Of course not. No one foresaw the necessity of bringing it. I am wearing purple because it suits me."

"Everything suits you!" Isobel retorted.

"No, it doesn't. Everything I wear suits me, because I have enough sense not to wear what doesn't. Now put on your armor, and come to dinner."

"Armor!"

"Courage, dignity, hope—and enough sense not to speak unless you are spoken to, and not to try to be funny."

"Funny! I couldn't laugh if Lord Salchester performed handstands on the lawn!"

"You could if Lady Warburton choked on the soup."

Isobel smiled wanly. "You're right," she agreed. "I could."

But dinner was a nightmare. Aside from Omegus, no one greeted Isobel. It was as if they had not seen her, even though she came down the great staircase, dark satins rustling, and the outswept edge of her skirts actually brushed those of Blanche Twyford because she did not move to allow her past. A moment later, as Vespasia passed, Blanche stepped aside graciously.

The conversation was free-flowing, but Isobel was not included. She spoke once, but no one appeared to hear her.

When the butler announced that dinner was served, Omegus offered her his arm, because it was apparent that no other man was going to. Once they were seated, Lady Warburton looked at Lady Vespasia, then at Omegus.

"Am I mistaken, Mr. Jones, or did you lay down the rules of this medieval trial of yours with the intention that we were all to be bound by them or our own honor was also forfeit?"

"I did, Lady Warburton," he replied.

"Then perhaps you would explain them to me again. You seem to be flouting what I understood you to say." She looked meaningfully at Isobel, then back again at Omegus with a wide challenging gaze.

He colored faintly. "You are right, Lady Warburton," he conceded. "I am as bound as anyone else, but I am still hoping that Mrs. Alvie will reconsider her refusal, and then a final decision must be made. I choose to wait until then before I act."

"I suppose you have that privilege," she said grudgingly. "At least while we are at Applecross."

The meal began, and Isobel was served exactly as everyone else was, but when she requested that the salt be passed to her, Fenton Twyford, who was next to her, looked across the table at Peter Hanning and asked his opinion on the likely winner of the Derby next year.

"Would you be kind enough to pass me the salt?" Isobel reiterated.

"I must say I disagree," Twyford said loudly in the silence. "I think that colt of Bamburgh's will take it. What do you think, Rosythe?"

Isobel did not ask again.

The rest of the meal proceeded in the same way. She was ignored as if her seat were empty. People spoke of Christmas, and of next year, who would attend what function during the season—the balls, races, regattas, garden parties, exhibitions, the opera, the theater, the pleasure cruises down the Thames. No one asked Isobel where she was going. They behaved as if she would not be there. There was no grief as if for the dead, as when Gwendolen's name was mentioned. It was not simply a ceasing to be, but as if she had never been.

She remained at the table, growing paler and paler. Vespasia walked beside her when the ladies withdrew to leave the gentlemen to their port. It was painful to remember that this time yesterday Gwendolen had been with them. None of the tragedy had happened. Now she was lying in one of the unused morning rooms, and tomorrow the undertaker would come to dress her for the grave.

Perhaps it was the closeness of the hour to the event, but as the women entered the withdrawing room, each one fell silent. Vespasia found herself shivering. Death was not a stranger to any of them. There were many diseases, the risks of childbirth, the accidents of even quite ordinary travel, but this was different, and the darkness of it touched them all.

Within twenty minutes of the door closing, Isobel rose to her feet, and since they had not acknowledged her presence, she did not bother to excuse her leaving. She went out in silence.

Vespasia followed almost immediately. Not only did she need to see Isobel and try in every way she could to persuade her to make the journey to Scotland, she felt she could not bear to stay any longer in the withdrawing room with the other women and observe their gloating. There was something repellent in their relishing of Isobel's downfall and the doling out of punishment, because it had nothing to do with justice, or the possibility of expiation. It was to do with personal safety and the satisfaction of being one of the included, not of those exiled.

Vespasia went back across the hallway, where she was greeted courteously by the butler. She wished him good night, wondering how awkward it was going to be for the domestic staff to work their way through the silences and rebuffs and decide whose leads to follow. Perhaps the real question was, how long would Omegus hold out against his own edict?

At the top of the stairs she retraced her path along the east wing and knocked on Isobel's door.

Again it was not answered, and again she went in.

Isobel was standing in the middle of the floor, her body stiff, her face white with misery. "Don't you ever wait to be invited?" Her husky voice was on the edge of losing control.

Vespasia closed the door behind her. "I don't think I can afford to wait," she replied.

Isobel took a deep breath, steadying herself with a visible effort. "And what can you possibly say that matters?" she asked.

Vespasia swept her considerable skirt to one side and sat down on the bedroom chair, as if she intended to stay for some time. "Do you intend to accept virtual banishment? And don't delude yourself that it will only be by those who are here this weekend, because it will not. They will repeat it all as soon as they return to London. By next season all society will have one version of it or another. If you are honest, you know that is true."

Isobel's eyes swam with tears, but she refused to give way to them. "Are you going to suggest that I accept the blame for Gwendolen's death and take this wretched letter to her mother?" she said, her voice choking. "All I did was imply that she was ambitious, which was perfectly true. Most women are. We have to be."

"You were cruel, and funny at her expense." Vespasia added the further truth. "You implied she was ambitious, but also that her love for Bertie would cease to exist were he in a different social or financial class."

Isobel's dark eyes widened. "And you are claiming that it would not? You believe she would marry a greengrocer? Or a footman?"

"Of course not," Vespasia said impatiently. "To begin with, no greengrocer or footman would ask her. The point is irrelevant. Your remark was meant to crush her and make her appear greedy and, more important, to make Bertie see her love for him as merely opportunism. Don't be disingenuous, Isobel."

Isobel glared at her, but she was too close to losing control to trust herself to speak.

"Anyway," Vespasia went on briskly. "None of it matters very much—"

"Is that what you intruded into my bedroom to tell me?" Isobel gasped, the tears brimming over and running down her cheeks. "Get out! You are worse than they are! I imagined you were my friend, and, my God, how mistaken I was! You are a hypocrite!"

Vespasia remained exactly where she was. She did not even move enough to rustle the silk of her gown. "What matters," she said steadily, "is that we face the situation as it is, and deal with it. None of them is interested in the truth, and it is unlikely we will ever know exactly why Gwendolen killed herself, far less prove it to people who do not wish to know. But Omegus has offered you a chance not only to expiate whatever guilt you might have, but to retain your position in society and oblige everyone here to keep absolute silence about it or face ostracism themselves—which is a feat of genius, I believe." She smiled slightly. "And if you succeed, you will have the pleasure of watching them next season, watching you and being unable to say a word. Lady Warburton and Blanche Twyford will find it extremely hard. They will suffer every moment of forced civility in silence. That alone should be of immeasurable satisfaction to you. It will be to me!"

Isobel smiled a little tremulously. She took a shuddering breath. "All the way to Inverness?"

"There will be trains," Vespasia responded. "The line goes that far now."

Isobel looked away. "That will be the least part of it. I daresay it will take days, and be cold and uncomfortable, with infinite stops. But facing that woman, and giving her Gwendolen's letter, which might say anything about me! And having to wait and watch her grief? It will be . . . unbearable!"

"It will be difficult, but not unbearable," Vespasia corrected.

Isobel stared at her furiously. "Would you do it? And don't you dare lie to me!"

Vespasia heard her own voice with amazement. "I will do. I'll come with you."

Isobel blinked. "Really? You promise?"

Vespasia breathed in and out slowly. What on earth had she committed herself to? She was not guilty of any offense toward Gwendolen Kilmuir. But had that really anything to do with it? Neither guilt nor innocence was really the issue. Friendship was—and need. "Yes," she said aloud. "I'll come with you. We shall set off tomorrow morning. We will have to go to London first, of course, and then take the next train to Scotland. We will deliver the letter to Mrs. Naylor, and we will accompany her back here if she will allow us to. Omegus said nothing about your journeying alone—merely that you had to go."

"Thank you," Isobel said, the tears running unchecked down her face. "Thank you very much."

Vespasia stood up. "We shall tell them tomorrow morning at breakfast. Have your maid pack, and dress for traveling. Wear your warmest suit and your best boots. There will probably be snow farther north, and it will be bound to be colder."

Vespasia's mind whirled with the enormity of her decision. When she finally fell asleep, her dreams were of roaring trains and windy snow-swept landscapes, and a grief-stricken and unforgiving woman bereft of her child.

She woke with a headache, dressed for travel, and left her maid packing while she went down to breakfast.

Everyone was assembled, ready to begin the new day's ostracism. The dining room was warm, the fire lit, and the sideboard laden with silver dishes from which delicious aromas emanated. Only Omegus looked distinctly unhappy. Almost immediately he caught Vespasia's eye, and she smiled at him, giving an imperceptible nod, and she saw the answering flash of light in his eyes. His body eased, and his right hand unclenched where it lay on the fresh linen of the table.

Isobel came in almost on Vespasia's heels, as if she had been waiting.

Everyone greeted Vespasia as effusively as they calculatedly ignored Isobel. This time she did not speak, but took her place at the table with a calm, pale face and began to eat after helping herself from the toast rack and the teapot.

Peter Hanning mentioned the weather and invited Bertie to a game of billiards in the afternoon. Lord Salchester announced that he was going for a walk. Lady Salchester said that she would accompany him, which took the smile from his face.

Isobel finished her toast and stood up, turning to Omegus.

"Mr. Jones, I have given your offer much serious thought. I was mistaken to refuse it. A chance to redeem oneself, and have past errors forgotten as if they had not existed, is something given far too rarely, and should not be declined. I shall leave Applecross this morning, taking the letter to Mrs. Naylor with me, and I shall catch the first available train to Scotland and deliver it to her. If she will accept my company on the return, then I shall do that also. When we reach London again, I shall inform you of the outcome, and trust that everyone here will keep their word according to our bond."

Lady Warburton looked crestfallen, as if she had lifted a particularly delicate morsel to her lips, only to have it fall onto the floor.

The ghost of a smile touched Isobel's face.

"How shall we know that you gave the letter to Mrs. Naylor, and did not merely say that you did?" Lady Warburton asked irritably.

"You will have Mrs. Alvie's word for it!" Omegus answered coldly.

"You will also have Mrs. Naylor's word, should you wish to ask her," Isobel pointed out.

"Really!" Lady Warburton subsided into indignant silence.

"Bravo," Lord Salchester said softly. "You have courage, my dear. It will not be a comfortable journey."

"It will be abysmal!" Fenton Twyford added. "Inverness could be knee-deep in snow, and the shortest day of the year is only three weeks away. In the far north of Scotland that could mean hardly any daylight at all. You do realize Inverness is another hundred and fifty miles north of Edinburgh, I suppose. At least!"

"What if your train gets stuck in a snowdrift?" Blanche asked hopefully.

"It is the beginning of December, not mid-January," Sir John Warburton pointed out. "It could be perfectly pleasant. Invernessshire is a fine county."

Lady Warburton looked surprised. "When were you ever there?"

He smiled. "Oh, once or twice. So was Fenton, you know."

"Doing what?"

"Wonderful country for walking."

"In December?" Hanning's eyebrows shot up, and his voice was sharp with disbelief.

"It hardly matters," Vespasia interrupted. "Now is when we are going. We shall leave as soon as our packing is completed—if the trap can be arranged to take us to the railway station."

"You are leaving, as well?" Lord Salchester said with clear disappointment.

Omegus looked at Vespasia.

"Yes," she replied.

Isobel smiled, pride in her face, and a shadow of

uncertainty. "Lady Vespasia has offered to come with me."

Omegus smiled, a sweet, shining look that lit his face, making him beautiful.

"To give the letter to Mrs. Naylor, if Mrs. Alvie should lose her nerve?" Blanche Twyford said bitingly. "That hardly makes of it the ordeal it is supposed to be!" She turned to Omegus. "Are we still bound by our oaths, in spite of this new turn of events?"

Omegus turned to her. "In the medieval trials of which I spoke, and upon which I have modeled my plan, the accused person was permitted friends to speak for them, and the friend risked facing the sure punishment along with them. If found guilty, the accused person promised to undertake the pilgrimage assigned, and if their friend were sure enough of their worth, had the courage and the selflessness to go with them, then that was the greatest mark of friendship that they could show. Neither the physical hardship nor the spiritual journey will be lessened, nor the threats that face them along the way. They will simply face them together, rather than alone. And the answer to your question, Mrs. Twyford, is, yes, you are just as bound."

Lord Salchester looked at Vespasia. "Remarkable," he said with very obvious admiration. "I admire your loyalty, my dear."

"Stubbornness," Lady Warburton said under her breath.

Bertie avoided eye contact with Isobel.

Vespasia looked at Omegus, who was regarding her with a happiness that she found suddenly and startlingly disconcerting. She wondered for a moment if she had made the rash promise for Isobel's sake, or just so she could see that look in Omegus's eyes. Then she dismissed it as absurd and finished her breakfast.

The ladies' maids would follow later with their luggage and remain at their respective houses in London. The expiatory journey was to be made alone. It would be both unfair and compromising to the integrity of the oath were the maids to have gone, as well. They did not deserve the hardship; nor were they party to any agreement of silence.

Vespasia and Isobel departed just after ten o'clock, with ample time to catch the next train to London. Omegus saw them off at the front door, his hair whipped by the fresh, hard wind that blew off the sweeping parkland with the clean smell of rain.

"I shall be waiting for your word from London," he said quietly. "I wish you Godspeed."

"Are you quite sure it is acceptable for Vespasia to

come with me? I have no intention of making this journey only to discover at the end that it doesn't count."

"It counts," he assured her. "Do not underestimate the difficulties ahead, just because you are not alone. Vespasia may ease some of it for you, both by her presence and her wit and courage, but it is you who must face Mrs. Naylor. Should she do that for you, then indeed you will not have made your expiation. If you should lie, society may forgive you, unable to prove your deceit, but you will know, and that is what matters in the end."

"I won't lie!" Isobel said stiffly, anger tight in her voice.

"Of course you will not," he agreed. "And Vespasia will be your witness, in case Mrs. Naylor is not inclined to be."

Isobel bit her lip. "I admit, I had not thought of that. I suppose it would not be surprising. I . . . I wish I knew what that letter said!"

His face shadowed. "You cannot," he said with a note of warning. "I am afraid that uncertainty is part of your journey. Now you must go, or you may miss the train. It is a long wait until the next one." He turned to Vespasia. "Much will happen to you before I see you again, my dear. Please God, the harvest of it will be good. Godspeed."

"Good-bye, Omegus," she answered, accepting his

hand to climb up into the trap and seat herself with the rug wrapped around her knees.

The groom urged the pony forward as Isobel clasped her hands in front of her, staring ahead into the wind, and Vespasia turned once to see Omegus still standing in the doorway, a slender figure, arms by his sides, but still watching them until they went around the corner of the driveway and the great elm tree trunks closed him from sight.

PART TWO

THE TRAIN JOURNEY TO LONDON SEEMED TE-
dious, but it was in fact very short, little more than
two hours, compared with the forthcoming journey
northward. In London they took separate hansoms to
their individual houses in order to pack more suitable
clothes for the next step. Evening gowns would not
be needed, and there would be no ladies' maids to
care for them. Additional winter skirts and heavier
jackets, boots, and capes were definite requisites.

Isobel and Vespasia agreed to meet at Euston Station preparatory to catch the northbound train at five
o'clock that afternoon. Vespasia arrived first, and
was angry with herself for being anxious in case Isobel at the last moment lost her nerve. She paced back
and forth on the freezing platform. Odd how railway
stations always seemed to funnel the wind until it in-
creased its strength and its biting edge to twice whatever it was anywhere else! And of course, the air was

full of steam, flying smuts of soot, and the noise—shouting, doors clanging to, and people coming and going.

Then fifteen minutes before the train was due to depart, she saw Isobel's tall figure sweeping ahead of a porter with her baggage, her head jerking from right to left as she searched for Vespasia, obviously afflicted by the same fear of facing the journey, and its more dreadful arrival, alone.

"Thank heaven!" she said, her voice shaking with intense relief as she saw Vespasia. She waved her arm at the porter. "Thank you! This will be excellent. Please put them aboard for me." And she opened her reticule to find an appropriate reward for him.

"Did you doubt me?" Vespasia asked her.

"Of course not!" Isobel said with feeling. "Did you doubt me?"

"Of course not!" Vespasia replied, smiling.

"Liar!" Isobel smiled back. "It's going to be awful, isn't it!" It was not a question.

"I should think so," Vespasia agreed. "Do you wish to turn back?"

Isobel pulled a rueful face, and there was honesty and fear in her eyes. "I would love to, but it would be worse in the end. Besides, I told those wretched people that I would. I sealed my fate then. Nothing this could do to me would be worse than facing them if I fail!"

"Of course. That was the whole purpose of saying

it at the breakfast table, surely?" Vespasia stopped the porter and added her financial appreciation as he loaded her luggage, as well, just one case, more and warmer clothes, in case they should be needed. If they were fortunate, the whole mission could be accomplished in two days, and they would be able to return. The long weekend at Applecross would be barely finished before they were in London again.

The train pulled out with whistles and clangs and much belching of steam. Slowly it picked up speed through the city, past serried rows of rooftops, then green spaces, factories, more houses, and eventually out into the open countryside, now patched with the dark turned earth of plowed fields and the scattered leafless copses of woodland. The rhythm of the wheels over the track would have been soothing, were they going anywhere else.

The winter afternoon faded quickly, and it was not more than an hour before they were rushing through the night, the steam past the window reduced to the red lines from lit sparks at speed, everything else a blur of darkness.

They stopped regularly, to set down passengers or to pick up more, and, of course, to allow people to stretch their legs, avail themselves of necessary facilities, and purchase refreshments of one sort or another.

Vespasia tried to sleep through as much of the night as she could. The movement of the train was pleasant and kept up a steady kind of music, but sitting more or less upright was far from comfortable. She was aware of Isobel watching the lights of stations and towns pass by with their steady progress northward, and knew she must dread their arrival. But they had exhausted discussion of the subject and Vespasia declined to be drawn into speculation any further.

Dawn came gray and windswept as they climbed beyond the Yorkshire moors to the bleaker and more barren heights of Durham, and then Northumberland, and at last on toward the border with Scotland. They purchased breakfast at one of the many stations and took it back to eat on the train as it pulled out again.

Vespasia determined not to return to the reason for their visit and talked instead of subjects that might ordinarily have aroused their interest—fashion, theater, gossip, political events. Neither of them cared just now, but Isobel joined in the fiction that everything was as usual.

As they crossed the Lowlands toward Edinburgh, the brooding and magnificent city that was Scotland's capital and seat of power and learning, the skies cleared, and it was merely briskly cold. They alighted and, with the help of a porter, took their luggage to await the train for the last hundred and fifty miles to Inverness.

An hour and a half later they were aboard, stiff, cold, and extremely tired, but again moving northward. As they came into Stirlingshire there was snow on the hills, but the black crown of Stirling Castle stood out against a blue sky with wind-ragged clouds streaming across it like banners.

The country grew wilder. The slopes were black with faded heather and the peaks higher and brilliant white against the sky. On the lower slopes they saw herds of red deer, and once what looked like an eagle, a dark spot circling in the sky, but it could have been a buzzard. The early afternoon was fading when at last they pulled into Inverness and saw the sprawl of sunset fire across the south, its light reflected paler on the sea. The mound of the Black Isle lay to the north, and beyond that, snow-gleaming mountains of Ross-shire and Sutherland.

The wind on the platform was like a scythe, cutting through even the best woolen clothing, and there was the smell of snow in it, and vast, clean spaces. It was an unconscious decision to find lodgings for the night rather than make any attempt to find Mrs. Naylor's house in the dark, in a town with which neither of them had the slightest familiarity. The station hotel seemed to offer excellent rooms, and had two available. The morning was soon enough to face the ultimate test.

Inquiry of the staff of the hotel elicited the information that the address on Gwendolen's letter was not actually in Inverness itself but was a considerable estate on the outskirts of Muir-of-Ord, a town some distance away, for which it would be necessary to hire a trap, and it would take a good part of the morning to reach it.

Thus it was actually close to midday when they finally reached the Naylor house, set on several acres of richly wooded land sweeping down to the Beauly Firth and ultimately the open sea.

Vespasia looked at Isobel. "Are you ready?" she asked gently.

"No, nor will I ever be," Isobel responded. "But then, I am so cold I am not even sure if I can stand on my feet, and whatever lies within that house, it cannot be less comfortable than sitting out here."

Vespasia wished profoundly that that would prove to be true, but she did not say so aloud.

They alighted, thanked the driver, and asked him to wait, in case they should not be invited to remain and have no way of returning to the town. Vespasia hung back and allowed Isobel to step forward and pull the bell knob beside the door. She was about to reach for it a second time, impatient to get the ordeal over, when it swung open and an elderly manservant looked at her inquiringly.

"Good morning," Isobel said, her voice catching with nervousness now that the moment was upon her. "My name is Isobel Alvie. I have come from London with a letter of importance to give to Mrs. Naylor. With me is my friend Lady Vespasia Cumming-Gould. I would be most grateful if you could give Mrs. Naylor that message, and apologize for my not having sent my card first, but the journey is urgent, and was unexpected." She offered him her card now.

"If you will come in, Mrs. Alvie, Lady Vespasia, I shall consider what is best to do," the man said in a soft northern accent.

Isobel hesitated. "What is best to do?" she repeated.

"Aye, madame. Mrs. Naylor is not at home, but I am sure she would wish you to receive the hospitality of the house. Please come in." He held the door wide for them.

Isobel glanced at Vespasia, then with a shrug so slight it was barely visible, she followed the manservant over the step and inside. Vespasia went after her into a large low-beamed hall with a fire blazing in an open hearth, then past it and into an informal sitting room with sunlight vivid through windows. A lawn sloped downward to a magnificent view beyond, but it was distinctly cooler.

"When do you expect Mrs. Naylor?" Isobel inquired. Her voice was rough-edged, and Vespasia could hear the tension in it.

"I'm sorry, madame, but I have no idea," the man said gravely. "I'm sorry you've traveled all this way an' we cannot help you."

"Where has she gone?" Isobel asked. "You must know!"

He looked startled at her persistence. It was discourteous, to say the least.

Vespasia stepped forward. She was not completing the task for Isobel, only ensuring that she had the opportunity to do it for herself. "I apologize if we seem intrusive," she said gently. "But there has been a tragedy in London, and it concerns Mrs. Naylor's daughter. We have to bring her news of it, no matter how difficult that may be. Please understand our distress and concern."

"Miss Gwendolen?" The man's face pinched with some emotion of pain, but it was impossible to read in it more than that. "Poor bairn," he said sadly. "Poor bairn."

"We must tell Mrs. Naylor," Vespasia said again. "And deliver the letter into her hands. It is a duty we have given our word to complete."

The man shook his head. "It's not another death, is it?" he asked, looking from one to the other of them, and back again.

Vespasia allowed Isobel to answer.

"Yes, I am terribly sorry to tell you, it is. So you see why we must speak to Mrs. Naylor in person. We were both there, and can at least tell her something of it, if she should wish to know."

"It'll be Miss Gwendolen herself this time," he said, shaking his head stiffly, his eyes bright and far distant.

Vespasia felt intrusive in his shock and sadness.

"Yes. I'm profoundly sorry," Isobel answered. "Where can we find her, or send a message so she may return, if that is what she would prefer? We are prepared to accompany her south, if she would permit us to."

"Aye, mebbe." He nodded awkwardly. "Mebbe. It's a long journey, and that's the truth."

"Yes, it is, but the train transfer in Edinburgh is not too inconvenient."

"Oh, lassie, there's no train from Ballachulish, and no likely to be in your lifetime, or your grandbairns', neither," he said with a sad little smile. "And mebbe that's for the best, too. Boat to Glasgow, it'll be. I've heard tell there's railways to Glasgow now." He spoke of it with an expression as if it were some exotic and far-distant Babylon.

"Ballachulish?" Isobel repeated uncertainly. "Where is that? How does one get there?"

"Oh, to Inverness, it'll be," he replied. "And then down the loch to the Caledonian Canal, and mebbe Fort William. Or else across Rannoch Moor and through Glencoe. Ballachulish lies at the end of it, so I'm told."

"How far is it?" Isobel obviously had no idea at all.

"Lassie, it's the other side o' Scotland! On the west coast, it is."

Isobel took a deep breath. "When will Mrs. Naylor be back?"

"That's it, you see," he said, shaking his head. "She

73

won't, least not so far as we know. It might be next spring, or then again it might not."

Isobel was horrified. "But that's . . . that's the other side of winter!"

"Aye, so it is. You're welcome to stay the night, while you think on it," he offered. "There's plenty of room. There's been barely a soul in the house since poor Mr. Kilmuir met his accident. It'll be good to have someone to cook for, and the sound of voices not our own."

"Has Mrs. Naylor been gone so long?" Vespasia put in with surprise. "I thought that was well over a year ago."

"Year and a half," he replied. "Early summer, it was, of '51. Now, if I can get you some luncheon, perhaps? You'll not have eaten, I'll be bound."

"Thank you," Vespasia accepted before Isobel could demur. They needed sustenance, and even more they needed the time it would take in order to make a decision in the face of this devastating news.

"What on earth are we going to do?" Isobel asked as soon as they were alone in the main hall again where the fire was warmer. "Will they listen if I explain to them that Mrs. Naylor wasn't here, and wherever she is, is at the other side of Scotland, and there's no way to get there?"

"No," Vespasia said frankly. "For a start, if she is there, then there must be a way for us to get there, also." But as she said it she felt panic well up inside her. She had spoken on impulse when she promised to come as far as Inverness with Isobel. Part of it was sympathy, part a profound and increasing dislike for Lady Warburton and a desire to see her thwarted, and a good deal more than she had realized before, a desire for Omegus's respect, even admiration. Now it was beginning to look like a far greater task than she had bargained for. But pride would not let her falter now, and honesty would not allow her to let Isobel believe that what they had done so far would satisfy their oath.

Isobel stared into the fire, her face set, jaw tight. "This is ridiculous! Why on earth did this wretched woman go across to the other side of the country? How did Gwendolen suppose anyone was going to get a letter to her? Nobody thought about that when they sent us on a wild-goose chase all the way up here!"

It was an implied criticism of Omegus, and Vespasia found it stung.

"Nobody sent us here," she replied. "It was an opportunity offered so you could redeem yourself from a stupid and cruel remark which ended in tragedy. Omegus did not cause any part of that."

Isobel swung around in her chair. "If Gwendolen had any courage at all, she would simply have answered me back! Not gone off and thrown herself into the lake! Or if she wanted to make a grand gesture, then she could at least have done it in the daytime, when someone would have seen her and pulled her out!"

"Sodden wet, her clothes clinging to her, her hair like rats' tails, covered in mud and weed? To do what, for heaven's sake?" Vespasia asked. "It may be romantic to fling yourself into the lake. It is merely ridiculous to be dragged out of it!" But as she stood up and walked away from Isobel toward the window looking over the long slope toward the sea, other thoughts stirred in her mind, memories of Gwendolen happy and with ever-growing confidence. Deliberately she then pictured the moment Isobel had spoken, the freezing seconds before anything had changed, and then Gwendolen's face stricken with horror. She did not understand it. It was out of proportion to the cruelty of the words. That Bertie did not defend her and then later did not even go after her to protest his disbelief of anything so shallow in her must have hurt her more than she could bear; it was the wound of disillusion. Perhaps she really had loved him and not seen his reality before.

She tried to recall Gwendolen all through the season. Had she really seemed so fragile? Image after image came to her mind. They were all ordinary, a young woman emerging from mourning, beginning to enjoy herself again, laughing, flirting a little, being careful with expenses, but not seemingly in any difficulty. But had Vespasia looked at her more than superficially?

For that matter, had she looked at Isobel more than as an intelligent companion, a little different from the ordinary, with whom it was agreeable to spend time, because she had opinions and did not merely say what was expected of her? Vespasia had not honestly sought anything more from her than a relief from tedium. She had told Isobel nothing of herself, certainly nothing of Rome. But she had told nobody of that.

How odd that Mrs. Naylor had left here so soon after Kilmuir's death, and apparently with no intention of returning. Something must have prompted such an extraordinary decision.

She turned and walked out of the hall into the corridor and along to the doorway at the end, which opened onto a gravel path. It was a bright day with a chill wind blowing off the water. The garden was beautifully kept, with grass smooth as a bowling green, perennial flowers clipped back, fruit trees carefully espaliered against the south-facing walls. She walked until she found a man coming from the kitchen garden, and complimented him on it. He thanked her solemnly.

"Mrs. Naylor must miss this very much," she said conversationally. "Is Ballachulish equally pleasant?"

"Och, it's very grand, and all that, with the mountains and the glen, and so on," he answered. "But the west is too wet for my liking. It's a land full of moods. Very dramatic. No much use for growing a garden like this."

"Why would one choose to live there?" How bold dare she be?

"There you have me, my lady," he confessed. "I couldn' a do it, and that's the truth. But if you're a west-coaster, it's different. They love it like it was woven into their skins."

"Oh? Mrs. Naylor is a west-coaster?" How simple after all.

"Not she! She's an Englishwoman like yourself," he said as if it surprised him, too. "She just took up and went there after poor Mr. Kilmuir was killed. Took it terrible hard. Mind, it was a bad thing, and so sudden, poor man."

"Yes, indeed," she said sympathetically, shivering a little as the wind knifed in over the water, ruffled and white-crested now. "Although I never heard exactly what happened. Poor Gwendolen was too shocked to speak of it."

"Horse bolted," he said, lowering his voice. "Kilmuir and Mrs. Naylor were out in the trap. He was thrown over by a branch, and got himself caught in the rein by his wrist."

"He was dragged?" she said in horror. "How appalling! No wonder Gwendolen could not speak of it! Poor Mrs. Naylor. She must have been frightened half out of her wits!"

"Och, no, madame, not she!" he said briskly, dismissing the very idea. "You do not know Mrs. Naylor if you could think that! More courage than any man I know! Any two men!" He lifted his head with fierce pride as he said it. He looked at her through furrowed brows. "You can smile, but it's true! Stopped the horse herself, but too late to help him, of course. Must have gone in the first moments. Cut the animal free and rode it home to tell us. Clear as day it was, when we found the wreckage, and poor Kilmuir."

"And Mrs. Kilmuir?" she asked.

He shook his head. "That's the worst of it, madame. She was out riding, and she saw the whole thing, but too far away to do anything but watch, like seeing your life coming to an end in front of your eyes." He shook his head minutely. "Didn't think she'd ever be the same again, poor child. Inconsolable, she was. Wandered around like a ghost, didn't eat a morsel, nor say a word to anyone. Glad we were when she finally went back to London, and word came that she'd started her life again, the poor lass."

"And Mrs. Naylor didn't go with her?"

His face stiffened and something within him closed. "No. She's no fondness for London, and too much to do up here. And if you'll be excusing me, my lady, I have to take these in for Cook to prepare dinner, since you and your friend will be staying. We'd like to treat you to our best, seeing as you're friends of Mrs. Kilmuir's. Walk in the garden all you will, and welcome."

She thanked him and continued on, but her mind was lost in picturing the death of Kilmuir, Mrs. Naylor's reaction, and her attempts to comfort a shattered daughter who had accidentally witnessed it all. She felt a consuming guilt that now they had to find Mrs. Naylor and tell her even worse news. The question of returning to London and simply leaving Gwendolen's letter to be found when she returned, whenever that was, had been irrevocably answered. It was unthinkable.

She told Isobel so when they were alone after dinner.

Isobel turned from the window where she had been standing before the open curtains, staring at the darkness and the water beyond. "Go down the Caledonian Canal, and then overland to Balla . . . whatever it is," she said in anguish. "How would we do that? Would anyone in their right mind at this time of year? Apart from sheepherders and brigands, that is!"

"Well, I shall try it," Vespasia responded. "If you wish to go back to London, then I am sure they will take you to Inverness. I shall go on at least as far as I can, and attempt to deliver the letter to Mrs. Naylor and tell her as much as I know of what happened."

Isobel's face was white, her eyes wide and angry. "That is moral blackmail!" she accused bitterly. "You know what they would say if I went back when you went on! It would be even worse for me than if I'd never come!"

"Yes, it probably would," Vespasia agreed. "So you will blackmail me into going back and leaving that poor woman to discover that her daughter is dead—whenever she returns here, this year, or next!"

Isobel blinked.

"We appear to have reached an impasse," Vespasia observed coolly. "Perhaps we should both do as we think right? I am going to Ballachulish, or as far toward it as I can. As you may have noticed, there is very little snow so far."

Isobel bit her lip and turned away. "You always get what you want, don't you?" she said quietly. Her voice was trembling, but it was impossible to tell if it was from anger or fear. "You have money, beauty, and a title, and by heaven, do you know how to use them!" And without looking back she swept out of the room, and Vespasia heard her steps across the hall.

Vespasia stood alone. Surely what Isobel said was not true? Was she so spoiled, so protected from the reality of other people's lives? Certainly she had great beauty; she could hardly fail to be aware of that. If the looking glass had not told her, then the envy of women and the adoration of men would have. It was fun; of course it was. But what was it worth? In a few years it would fade, and those who valued her for that alone would leave her for the new beauty of the day—younger, fresher.

And, yes, she had money. She admitted she was unfamiliar with want for any material thing. And a title? That, too. It opened all manner of doors that would always be closed to others. Was she spoiled? Was she without any true imagination or compassion? Did she lack strength, because she had never been tested?

No, that was not true! Rome had tested her to the last ounce of her strength. Isobel would never know what she would have given to stay there with Mario, whatever their ideological differences, his republicanism and her monarchist loyalty, his revolutionary passion and fire and her belief in treasuring old and beautiful ways that had proved good down the centuries. Over it all towered his laughter, his warmth, his courage to live or die for his beliefs. How unlike the ordinary, pedestrian kindness of her husband, who gave her freedom but left her soul empty.

However, that was nothing to do with Isobel, and she would never know of it. This was her journey of expiation, not Vespasia's.

*T*hey set out immediately after breakfast, Mrs. Naylor's household providing them with transport by pony and trap as far as Inverness and then beyond to the eastern end of Loch Ness, where they could hire a boat. It would take them the length of the long, winding inland lake with its steep mountainsides as if it were actually a great cleft in the earth filled with fath-

omless satin gray water, bright as steel. All the way
there they had spoken barely a word to each other,
sitting side by side in the trap, the wind in their faces,
rugs wrapped tightly around their knees.

"It's a good thirty mile to Fort Augustus, so it is,"
the boatman said as they embarked. He shook his
head at the thought. "Then there's the canal, and another good thirty mile o' that, before you reach Fort
William on the coast." He squinted up at the sky.
"And they always say in the west that if you can see
the hills, it'll rain as sure as can be."

"And if you can't?" Isobel asked.

"Then it's raining already." He smiled.

"Then we'd best get started," she answered briskly.
"Since it is a fine day now, obviously it is going to
rain!"

"Aye," he acknowledged. "If that's what you want?"

Without looking at Vespasia, Isobel repeated that it
was, and accepted the boatman's assistance into the
stern of the small vessel, most of it open to the elements. It was the only way in which they could begin
their journey.

They pulled out into the open water, but stayed
closer to the northern shore, as if the center might
hold promise of sudden storm, and indeed several
times squalls appeared out of nowhere. One moment
everything was dazzling with silver light on the water,
the slopes of the mountains vivid greens. Then out of
the air came a darkness, the peaks were shrouded,

and the distance veiled over with impenetrable sheets of driving rain.

They sheltered in the tiny cabin as the boat rocked and swung, flinging them from side to side. They said nothing, so cold their limbs shook, teeth clenched together. Vespasia cursed her own pride for coming, Isobel for her cruel tongue, Omegus for his redeeming ideas, and Gwendolen for wanting a shallow man like Bertie Rosythe and falling to pieces when she realized what he was.

"Do you suppose Gwendolen was still in love with Kilmuir?" Vespasia asked when they finally emerged into a glittering world, the water a flat mirror, burning with light in the center, mountains dark as basalt above, and drifts of rain obscuring in the distance.

Isobel looked at her in surprise. "You mean she realized it that evening, and the grief of losing him returned to her?" There was a lift of hope in her voice.

"Did you know her, other than just socially during the season?" Vespasia questioned.

Isobel thought for a few moments. They passed a castle on the foreshore, its outline dramatic against the mountains behind. "A little," she answered. "I know there was a sadness in her under the gaiety on the surface. But then she was a widow. I know what that is like. Whether you loved your husband wildly or not, there is a terrible loneliness at times."

Vespasia felt a stab of guilt. "Of course there must be," she said gently. It was not Isobel's right to know that it afflicted her, also—a different kind of loneliness, a hunger that had never been fed, except in brief, dangerous moments, a shared cause, a time that could never have lasted.

"Actually I thought Kilmuir was a bit of a cad," Isobel went on thoughtfully. "I'm not sure that he was any better than Bertie Rosythe, really. But it's natural to remember only what was good about someone after they are dead."

Vespasia studied Isobel's face and saw doubt in it and something that looked like guilt as she stared across the bright water with its shifting patterns, and not once after that did she look back at Vespasia, nor raise the subject again.

They stayed the night ashore, and continued the next day, reaching Fort Augustus by evening. They parted from that boat and set out on the canal at sunrise in another. The biting cold, the sense of claustrophobia on the long, narrow boat, and the knowledge that they were moving ever farther from land familiar to them, even by repute, eased some of the tension between them.

But above all was the dread of meeting Mrs. Naylor and having to tell her the truth. They spoke, to break the silence of the vast land and the strangeness of the situation. They sat closer to each other to keep a little warmth, and they shared food when it was offered them, and laughed self-consciously at the inconvenience of the requirements of nature. They filled the long tedium of waiting for lochs to fill or empty, stretching their legs by walking back and forth in the bitter wind, staring at the white-crowned hills.

Some time after dark on the fourth day from Inverness they arrived in Fort William, and again found lodgings. They were shivering with cold and exhaustion, and wretched beyond even thinking of how to move on from there to Ballachulish. They huddled by the fire, trying to get warm enough to think of sleep.

"Why, in the name of heaven, would Mrs. Naylor come here at all?" Isobel said wretchedly, rubbing her hands together and holding them out before the flames. "Let alone stay for a year and a half? No wonder Gwendolen never mentioned her. She was probably terrified in case anyone discovered she was insane!"

"Did she never mention her?" Vespasia asked, although Isobel's remark was sensible enough. She had wondered herself why Mrs. Naylor was not living in her very attractive house at Muir-of-Ord. If one wished seclusion, that was surely far enough from most society.

"Never," Isobel said frankly. "Which you must admit is unusual."

A new realization came to Vespasia. She had not appreciated before that Isobel had known Gwendolen so well that such an omission would be noticeable to her. In fact, there was rather a lot that Isobel had not said, but perhaps her own desire for Bertie

Rosythe's affection was deeper than it had seemed at Applecross.

"Yes," Vespasia said aloud. "Yes, it is." Actually she wondered why Mrs. Naylor had not come to London with Gwendolen to chaperone her and give all the help she could in gaining a second husband as soon as it was decent to do so.

"Exactly." Isobel tried to move her chair even closer to the fire, then realized that it would place her feet practically in the hearth, and her skirts where a spark might catch them, and changed her mind. "I'm dreading meeting this woman." She looked up at Vespasia candidly. "Do you suppose she might actually be dangerous?"

Vespasia weighed in her mind the need to continue their journey to the end, wherever that might be, and her growing hunger to know the truth of Gwendolen's reason for taking her own life. She was becoming concerned that what they had seen at Applecross was only a small part of it. The more she considered it, the less did it seem a sufficient reason.

"I suppose it is possible," she answered. "What did Gwendolen say about her family, if she did not speak of her mother at all?"

"Very little. It was all Kilmuir, and I suppose even that was only how much she missed him." Isobel frowned. "Naturally, she did not speak of the event of his death, but one would not expect her to. It would have been in very poor taste, distressing for her and embarrassing for everyone else." She shivered again and wrapped her cloak more tightly around her shoulders. "I have to confess, she behaved as I think I would have myself in that. I cannot fault her. It is simply odd that with a mother still living she never referred to her at all. However, if she's quite deranged, it would explain it completely." She puckered her brow. "Do we really have to continue until we find her?"

"Do you wish to turn back?"

Isobel pulled a rueful little face. "I wished to turn back as soon as we left Applecross, but not nearly as much as I do now. But I suppose since we have come this far, I should hate to have it all be in vain." She smiled and her eyes were bright for a second. "When it gets unbearably cold, miserable, and far from anything even remotely like home, I think of how furious Lady Warburton and Blanche Twyford will be if I complete this and they are obliged to forgive me, and it gives me courage to go on."

Vespasia knew exactly what she meant. The thought of Lady Warburton being charming because she had no choice had warmed her frozen body and put new vigor in her step more than once.

She smiled. "What was he like, Kilmuir?"

Isobel turned away, a shadow falling between her and Vespasia again, as clearly as if it had been visible. "I don't know."

"Yes, you do," Vespasia insisted. "You knew

Gwendolen far longer, and far better, than you have allowed me to suppose."

Isobel stared at her, her dark eyes wide and challenging. "If I did, why is that your concern? I am going to do my penance. Is that not enough for you? You, of all people, can see what a bitter thing it is!" She took a sudden sharp breath. "Is that actually why you are here, to make sure I do it all? Is that why Omegus Jones sent you?"

Vespasia was taken aback. The accusation was so unjust it caught her completely by surprise. "I came because I thought the journey could be long and hard, possibly even dangerous, and the ending of it the most difficult of all, and that you might surely need a friend," she answered. "Had I been making it, I should not have wished to do it alone. And Omegus did not send me."

Shame filled Isobel's face. "I'm sorry," she said huskily. "I have not ever been that sort of a friend to anyone. I find it hard to believe you could do it for me. Why should you? I . . . I don't think I would do it for you." She looked away. "Not that you would ever need it, of course."

Vespasia was tempted to answer her with truth, even to tell her some of the weight she carried within her, which was not only loneliness but, if she were honest, guilt as well, and fear. She had buried her memories of Rome, of passion, of the inner joy of not being alone in her dreams. Deliberately she had forced herself not to think of talking with someone who understood her words even before she said them, who filled one hunger even as he awoke others. She had refused to look at remembrance of the exhilaration of fighting with all her time and strength for a cause she believed in. She had returned to duty, to a round of social chitchat about a hundred things that did not matter and never had. She was now sitting with Isobel, whom she knew so little of, and who knew her even less. They were sharing the outward hardships of a journey, with an uncrossable gulf between them on the inner purpose of it. She had no crusade anymore. She had no battle to fight except against boredom, and there was no victory at the end of it, only another day to fill with pastimes that nourished nothing inside her.

"You have no idea whether I would or not," she said quietly. "You know nothing about me, except what you see on the outside, and that is mostly whatever I wish you to see, as it is with all of us."

Isobel looked startled. It had never occurred to her that Vespasia was anything more than the perfect beauty she seemed.

The fire was burning low. The wind battered the rain against the glass and whined in the eaves. Unless it eased, the boat journey down the loch to Ballachulish was going to be rough and unpleasant, but at this time of the year it would be days if not weeks before there was another fine, still day. Waiting for it was not a choice.

Isobel seemed lost in thought, overcome by new, previously unimagined ideas.

"Why did you say what you did to Gwendolen?" Vespasia asked. "You half implied that her choice somehow lay between servants and gentlemen, and she chose gentlemen for reasons of money and ambition."

Isobel blushed. It was visible even in the dying firelight. It was several moments before she answered, and she did not look at Vespasia even then. "I know it was cruel," she said softly. "I suppose that's why I'm really making this ridiculous journey. Otherwise, when we got to Inverness and found Mrs. Naylor wasn't home, I might have posted the letter and said I had done my best." She gave a little shudder. "No— that's not true. I'm doing it because I know I won't survive in society if I don't, and I have nowhere else to go, nowhere else I know how to behave or what to do."

"The reason?" Vespasia prompted.

Isobel lifted one shoulder in half a shrug. "Gossip. Stupid, I expect, but I heard it in more than one place."

Vespasia waited. "That is only half an answer," she said at last.

Isobel chewed her lip. "Everyone turns a blind eye if a man beds a handsome parlor maid or two, as long as he is reasonably discreet about it. A woman who was known to have slept with a footman would be ruined. She would be branded a whore. Her husband would disown her for it, and no one would blame him."

Vespasia could hardly believe it. "Are you saying Gwendolen Kilmuir slept with a footman? She must be insane! Far madder than her mother!"

Isobel looked at her at last. "No, I'm not saying she did, simply that there were rumors. Actually I think Kilmuir started them." She shut her eyes as if twisted by some deep, internal pain. "He was paying rather a lot of attention to Dolly Twyford, Fenton's youngest sister."

"I thought she wasn't married!" Vespasia was incredulous. There was a convention in certain circles: Once one had borne the appropriate children to one's husband, a married woman might then indulge her tastes, and as long as she did not behave with such indiscretion that it could not be overlooked, no one would chastise her for it. However, for a man to have an affair with a single woman was quite another thing. That would ruin her reputation and make any acceptable marriage impossible for her.

"She wasn't," Isobel agreed. "That was the whole point. The suggestion was that Gwendolen's conduct was so outrageous he would divorce her, and then after a suitable period, not very long, he would marry Dolly."

"Were they in love?"

"With what?" Isobel raised her eyebrows. "Dolly wanted a position in society, and the title probably coming to Kilmuir, and he wanted children. He had been married to Gwendolen for six years, and there were none so far. He was growing impatient. At least, that was the gossip." Her voice dropped. "And I knew it."

Vespasia did not answer. To say that it did not matter would be a dishonesty that would serve no one. Some penance was due for such a cruelty, and they were both deeply aware of it. But more than that, her mind was racing over the new picture of Gwendolen as it emerged now. Had Bertie Rosythe heard the gossip, as well, and was that the truth of why he had not gone after her and reassured her of his love? Or worse than that, had he gone and, far from offering her any comfort, made it plain that he had no intentions toward her? Did she see herself as ruined, not only for him but for any marriage at all?

Or worse even than that, could such rumors be true? Which raised the bitterly ugly question of whether Kilmuir's death had been a highly fortunate accident for Gwendolen, releasing her from the possibility of a scandalous divorce, from which her reputation would never have recovered. Instead she had become a widow, with everyone's sympathy, and excellent prospects in time of marrying again. How fortunate for her that it had been Mrs. Naylor who had been with him in the carriage, and not Gwendolen herself.

They discussed it no more. The fire was fading, and sleep beckoned like comforting arms. They were both happy to go upstairs and sink into oblivion until the morning should require them to face the elements and attempt to reach Ballachulish.

*I*t was a hard journey, even though not long as the crow or the gull were to fly. The sharp west wind obliged the little boat to tack back and forth down the coast through choppy seas, and both Isobel and Vespasia were relieved to put ashore at last in the tiny town of Ballachulish and feel the earth firm beneath their feet. They crossed the road from the harbor wall, heads down against the sleet, wind gusting, tearing skirts, and made their way to the inn. They asked the landlord about Mrs. Naylor, and his response brought them close to despair.

"Och, I'm that sorry to tell ye, but Mistress Naylor left Ballachulish nigh on a year ago!" he told them with chagrin.

"Left?" Isobel could scarcely believe it. "But she can't! Her household in Inverness told us she was here!"

"Aye, and so she was," he agreed, nodding. "But she left a year ago this Christmas. Grand lady, she was. Never knew any lady of such spirit, for all that she was as English as you are."

Isobel swallowed. "Where did she go? Do you know?"

"Aye, I do. Up through the Glen and over the moor to the Orchy. You'll no be going that way, though, till May or so. Even then it's a wild journey. Horses you'll need. The High Road passes right around there, and then south."

Isobel looked at Vespasia, the first signs of defeat in her eyes.

Vespasia felt a rush of pity, first for Isobel, knowing what awaited her in London if she failed. They would not care what the reason was, or if they could or would have done differently themselves. They were looking for excuses, and any would serve. Then she felt for Mrs. Naylor. However mad she was, whatever reason had brought her here and then driven her to go up into Glencoe and beyond, she still deserved to be told about her daughter's death face-to-face, not in a letter half a year late.

"I accept that it may be difficult," she said to the landlord. "Is it possible, with good horses and a guide?"

The man considered for several seconds. "Aye," he said at last. "Ye'll be used to riding, I take it?"

Vespasia looked at Isobel. She had no idea of the answer.

Isobel nodded. "Certainly. I've ridden in London often enough."

"Ye'll be needing a guide," he warned.

"Naturally," Vespasia agreed. "Would you arrange one for us, at whatever you consider a fair rate?"

Isobel blinked, but she made no demur.

*S*o it was that the next morning they set out in the company of a grizzled man by the name of MacIan, with a strong Highland pony each to ride, and three more to follow with luggage, water, and food.

"Keep close!" MacIan warned, fixing them in turn with a skeptical eye. "I'll no have time to be nurse-maiding ye, so if ye're in trouble, call out, don't just sit there and hope I'll be noticing, 'cause I won't. I've my work to keep these ponies on the track, not to speak of finding it mysel', if the weather turns." He cocked his head to one side and looked up at the wild sky with clouds racing across it casting the hills in brilliant light one moment, then shrouded in purple, and then black the next. The water in the loch was white-ruffled. The wind was laden with salt and the sharp smell of weed. It was ice-cold on the skin, whipping the blood up.

Isobel looked at Vespasia. For once they understood each other perfectly. Pride kept them from turning back. "Of course," they both agreed, and when MacIan was satisfied that they meant it, they set out of the village on the rough road through ever-steepening mountains toward the great Glen of the most treacherous massacre in the history of Scotland. In the winter of 1692 the Campbell guests had risen in the night and slain their MacDonald hosts—man, woman, and child—all in the cause of loyalty to the Hanoverian king from the south.

They rode in silence, because no conversation was possible. The wind tore their breath away, even if the labor of riding in single file along the track and the grandeur of the scenery had not robbed them of the wish to frame words for it.

At about one o'clock they stopped for something to eat, but primarily to rest the ponies. They were slightly sheltered by a buttress of rock, and Vespasia leaned against it and stared around her. On every side jagged mountains soared into the sky. Some were dark with heather on the lower slopes, the peaks like white teeth in the giant, upturned skull of some vast creature left behind from the beginning of time. The smell of the snow whetted the edge of the wind. It was a land of golden eagles and red deer, pools of peat-dark water, avalanches, and blizzards. There was a majesty, a terror, and a beauty that burned itself into the soul.

They remounted and set off again, climbing higher as the valley rose and the sides became steeper yet. Darkness fell early, and they stopped at a small hut, almost invisible in the dusk, amid the rock outcrops. It offered little hospitality beyond shelter from the elements, both for them and for the ponies. Vespasia was glad of that. She would not have left any creature out in the storm that was threatening, let alone beasts upon whom their lives might depend.

"Mrs. Naylor must be a raving madwoman," Isobel said grimly, settling down to sleep in her clothes. The only concession to comfort was to take the pins out of her hair. "And I'm beginning to think we are, too."

Vespasia was obliged to agree with her. The longer this journey continued, the more concerned she became as to what manner of woman Mrs. Naylor might be, and increasingly now, what had been the truth of the marriage between Gwendolen and Kilmuir, and exactly how he had died. Why had Gwendolen never spoken of her mother? What was the reason for what looked unmistakably like an estrangement?

Neither of them slept well. It was too cold and the wooden bunks were hard. It was a relief when daylight came and they could rise, eat a breakfast of oatmeal and salt, and drink hot tea, without milk, then continue on their way.

Outside was a staggering world. It had snowed during the night and the sky had cleared. The light was blinding. Sun glittered on ribbons of water cascading down the rock faces, hitting stones and leaping up, foaming white. An eagle drifted on the wind, a black speck against the blue.

They rode all day, resting only briefly for the ponies' sake. Vespasia was so tired from the unaccustomed exercise that every bone and muscle in her body ached, and she knew Isobel must feel the same, but neither of them would admit it. It was not that they imagined they were deceiving anyone, least of all MacIan; it was simply a matter of self-mastery. One complaint or admission would lead to another, and then perhaps thoughts of surrender. Once suggested, it would become a possibility, and that must not be permitted. The temptation was too powerful. Instead they concentrated on a few yards at a time, from here to the next turn in the track, the next stretch ahead.

Then just before dusk, as the sun was setting in shards of fire almost due south, the valley opened out and the great width of Rannoch Moor lay in front of them, dark-patched with heather and peat bogs, pools shining bronze in the dying light. In the distance of the sky, turquoise drifted into palest blue before the advancing shades of the night.

No one spoke, but Vespasia wondered if perhaps

Mrs. Naylor were not so mad after all. This was a different kind of sanity, undreamed of in London.

They found shelter again, but it was bitterly cold, and by morning the aches that had been slight the previous day were now sharper and reminded them of pain with every movement. It required all the concentration Vespasia could muster just to stay on her pony and watch where she was going. Her head ached from clenching her teeth, and she was stiff with cold. Not to complain had become a matter of honor, almost a reason for survival.

Clouds appeared on the horizon, billowing, burning with light, as if there had been an explosion just beyond their vision. Then hard on their heels came the squall, driving rain turning to sleet, pellets of ice that stung the skin. They bent into it, heads down, and kept going. There was nothing to break the strength of it, nothing to hide behind. They moved carefully, one step at a time.

It cleared again just as suddenly, and they were able to increase speed.

"We need to be in Glen Orchy by night," MacIan said grimly. "There's no place to rest before then, and the Orchy's no river to be stopping near, if ye've no house nor bothy to protect you."

Vespasia did not bother to ask why not; her imagination supplied a dozen answers. She was beginning to feel as if whatever Mrs. Naylor was like, it was going to be a blessed relief to find her and discharge their duty. It could hardly be worse than this. It had assumed nightmare properties. Perhaps the Vikings were right and hell was endless cold, a howling wind, a journey that never arrived anywhere, aching bones and muscles, and always the need to press onward.

Except surely hell could never be so soul-rendingly beautiful?

She saw Isobel sway in the saddle ahead of her, and more than once she was afraid she would fall herself, but by dusk they saw lights ahead of them. It seemed another endless, excruciating hour before they reached them and found them to be the windows of a large house, far greater in size than that for a single family.

Someone must have seen them come, because the door opened wide as their ponies' hooves clattered in the yard, and a large man with a storm-weathered face stood holding a lantern high.

"Well, MacIan, is it you, then? And what are you doing out on a night like this? Who is it you have with you? Ladies, is it? Well, come on inside then. I'll send Andrew and Willie out to tend to your ponies."

"Aye, Finn, it's a dreich night now," MacIan agreed cheerfully, climbing out of the saddle in an easy movement and turning back to help first Isobel and then Vespasia to the ground. Vespasia was horrified to discover she could barely stand up, and but for MacIan's hand, she would have staggered and lost her balance.

The door was held wide, and two young men

passed her, nodding shyly on their way to tend to the animals. Inside was blessedly warm. She was dizzy with relief. It was not until she had taken off her wet outer clothes and dried her face on the clean, rough towel handed her that she turned to see the woman standing in the doorway and regarding her with interest. She was tall, easily as tall as Vespasia, with auburn hair wound carelessly on her head, simply as had been convenient. She wore rough wool clothes, quite obviously designed for warmth and convenience of movement. Her face was wide-eyed, intelligent, handsome in a unique and highly individual way. Before she spoke, Vespasia knew that this was Mrs. Naylor.

She turned to Isobel, who seemed frozen, as if now that the moment had come, she could not find the courage. Crossing the moor had cost all she had.

Vespasia stepped forward. "Mrs. Naylor? My name is Vespasia Cumming-Gould." She indicated Isobel. "My friend Isobel Alvie. I apologize for arriving without permission at this hour. We had not realized quite what traveling from Inverness would involve."

"Beatrice Naylor," the woman answered, a definite smile on her lips. "No one does, the first time. But it is an experience that remains indelibly in the mind. What brings you to the Orchy, in December? It has to be of the utmost importance."

Vespasia turned to Isobel. They had already set foot through the door. Could they accept this woman's hospitality, even on a night like this, at the end of the earth, by answering her question with a lie?

Isobel's face was flushed from the sudden warmth inside, but white around the eyes and lips. The final moment of testing had come, the last and the greatest, upon which all the rest depended.

Vespasia realized she was holding her breath, her hands clenched at her sides. She could not help. If she did, she would rob Isobel forever of the chance to earn her redemption.

Mrs. Naylor was waiting.

"Yes, it is of the utmost importance," Isobel said at last, her words half-swallowed, her voice trembling. "I have never found anything harder in my life than bringing you the news that your daughter Gwendolen is dead. And I am bitterly ashamed that I contributed to the circumstances which brought it about." She held out the envelope. Traveling had bent it a little, but it remained sealed. "This is the letter she wrote to you."

The man who had opened the door to them moved silently to Mrs. Naylor and put his arm around her, holding her steady. He did it as naturally as if physical contact between them were understood. There was a great tenderness in his face, but he did not speak.

The silence stretched until the pain in it was a tangible thing in the room.

"I see," Mrs. Naylor said at last. "How did it happen?" She stared at Isobel with huge, almost unblinking eyes, as if she could read everything that was in Isobel's mind and beneath it, in the search for a truth she would rather not look at, even herself.

Isobel struggled to tear her gaze away, and failed. "At Applecross," she began, falteringly. "It was a long weekend house party, rather more of a week. I don't know if—"

"I am perfectly acquainted with weekend house parties, Mrs. Alvie," Mrs. Naylor said coldly. "You do not need to explain society or its customs to me. How did my daughter die, and what cause have you to blame yourself? I might think you spoke only as a manner of expressing your sympathy, but I can see in your face that you are in some very real way responsible." She looked briefly at Vespasia. "Does this include you also, Lady Vespasia? Or are you here simply as chaperone?"

Vespasia was startled that Mrs. Naylor knew of her, as the use of her title made clear. "Mrs. Alvie felt the duty to tell you herself, regardless of what the journey involved," she answered. "It is not one a friend would permit her to attempt alone."

"Such loyalty . . . ," Mrs. Naylor murmured. "Or do you share the blame?"

"No, she doesn't," Isobel cut in. "It was I who made the remark. Lady Vespasia had nothing to do with it."

Mrs. Naylor blinked. "The remark?"

Finn made a movement to interrupt, but Mrs. Naylor held up her hand peremptorily. "I will hear this! You know me better than to imagine I will faint or otherwise collapse. Tell me, Mrs. Alvie, how did my daughter die?"

Isobel drew a deep, shivering breath. They were all still standing in the big hallway, relieved only of their outer and wettest clothing. No one had yet eaten a morsel.

"She went out after darkness, when the rest of us had retired, and threw herself from the bridge across the end of the ornamental lake," Isobel answered. "We learned it only the next morning, when it was too late."

Finn grasped Mrs. Naylor by both arms, but she did not stagger or lean back against him. Her face was ashen white. "And in what way were you to blame, Mrs. Alvie?" she asked.

No one in the room moved. There was to be no mercy.

"We all believed that Bertie Rosythe would propose marriage to her that weekend," Isobel said hoarsely, her voice a dry rustle in the silence. "I made a cruel remark to the effect that she would not have loved him, had he been penniless or a servant. I made it from envy, because I also am a widow and had hoped to remarry, possibly to Bertie." She took a deliberate, shuddering breath. "I had no idea it would cause her such distress, but I accept that it did. Apparently he did not go after her to tell her that he knew it was nonsense. I . . . I am deeply ashamed." She did not look away but remained facing Mrs. Naylor.

"You do not need to tell me why you chose that particular barb," Mrs. Naylor said quietly, her voice brittle, every word falling with clarity. "Your face betrays that you heard the rumors and knew the weakness in her armor. Please don't let yourself down by denying it."

The tears stood out in Isobel's eyes. "I wasn't going to," she answered. Vespasia wondered if that were true, and was glad it had not been put to the test. She hated standing here helplessly, but to be of any value, this had to play itself out to the bitter end.

"Who else is aware of this?" Mrs. Naylor asked.

"No one, so far as I am aware," Isobel answered. "Except Lady Vespasia."

Mrs. Naylor turned to Vespasia.

"That is true," Vespasia told her. "Mr. Omegus Jones arranged that she should be buried privately—in the chapel in his grounds, by a minister he knows who would regard it as an accident. If we brought you the news, in person, those others present at Applecross that weekend are bound by oath to say nothing of what happened which would challenge that account."

"Really? And why would they do that?" Mrs. Naylor asked skeptically. "Society loves a scandal. Was it a group of saints you had there?" Her voice was hard-edged with grief and bitter past experience.

"No," Vespasia answered before Isobel could. She moved a fraction forward toward the center of the room, commanding Mrs. Naylor's attention. "They were very ordinary, self-regarding, ambitious, fragile people, just like those it seems you already know. They regarded Mrs. Alvie as to blame and were ready to ruin her, with that certain degree of pleasure that comes when you can do so with an excuse of self-righteousness."

Mrs. Naylor's face twisted at the memory, but she did not interrupt. Vespasia had her complete attention. The rest of the room, Finn, the fire crackling in the hearth, the wind beating against the window need not have existed.

"Mr. Jones proposed a trial, the verdict of which was to bind us, upon our oath," Vespasia went on. "Whoever was found guilty should undertake a journey of expiation, which if completed, would wash out the sin. If they failed, then everyone else was free to ostracize them completely. But if they succeeded, then anyone who referred to it afterward, for any reason public or private, should themselves meet with that same ostracism."

"How very clever," Mrs. Naylor said softly. "Your Mr. Jones is a man of the greatest wisdom. Expiation? I like that word. It conveys far more than punishment, or even repayment. It is a cleansing. Am I bound by this also?" She turned to Isobel, then back to Vespasia.

"You cannot be," Vespasia answered, seeing the one ghastly flaw in Omegus's plan. "You were not party to the oath." She smiled faintly, like a ghost. "And it does not seem you would be greatly affected if society did not speak to you. I find it difficult to imagine you would know, let alone care."

"You are quite right," Mrs. Naylor agreed. "But this is sufficient explanation for tonight. You have ridden far, and in inclement weather. We have food aplenty and room to spare. And your ponies need rest, whether you do or not." She looked at Isobel. "It will perhaps be harder for you to accept my hospitality than it will be for me to give it, but there is none other for miles around, so you had best learn to do it. Jean will find you rooms and food. I wish to retire and read my daughter's last letter to me." And she took Finn's arm and went out, neither of them turning to look behind.

Isobel and Vespasia had no alternative but to follow Jean, a silent, buxom woman, to where she offered them food and rooms for the night. When they were settled, with the luggage placed conveniently for them, Isobel came to Vespasia's door and accepted instantly the invitation to come in. Her face was pale, her dark eyes shadowed with misery.

"I'd almost rather sleep on the moor!" she said

wretchedly. "She knows that! What do you think she'll do tomorrow? Can we leave?"

"No. It is part of our oath that we accompany her to London, if she will allow us to," Vespasia reminded her.

Isobel closed her eyes, her fists clenched by her sides. "I don't think I can! Seven hundred miles, or more, with that woman! That is more punishment than I deserve, Vespasia. I said something stupid, a dozen words, that's all!"

"Cruel," Vespasia reminded her quietly, then wished she had been less blunt. It was not necessary. Isobel was perfectly aware of her fault. Vespasia had no right to demand proof of it every time. "And apart from finishing the task," she said more gently, "I am not at all sure that we can leave here without Mrs. Naylor's assistance. Do you have the faintest idea how to? I don't even know where we are, do you?"

"I must be mad!" Isobel was close to despair. "You're right. I expect MacIan is on her side, and most certainly Finn is. Who is he, anyway? For that matter, what is this place, and what in the name of heaven is Mrs. Naylor doing here? Apart from apparently living in sin!"

Vespasia ignored the gibe. "I don't know," she said. "But it is an interesting question. Why would a wealthy woman in her middle years choose to spend her time not only a great distance from the rest of society of any sort, but a virtually impossible distance?

In fact, why did she not return to London after Kilmuir's death, when Gwendolen did? It would be the most natural thing to do."

"The only answer is that there was an estrangement," Isobel answered. "Perhaps she will not wish to return to London, with us or alone."

"Sleep on the thought, if you wish," Vespasia said dryly. "But do not hold it longer than tomorrow morning." She gave her a smile with as much warmth in it as she could find strength for. "We shall surmise it," she added. "Just think of Lady Warburton's face. She will be fit to spit teeth."

Isobel forced herself to smile back, recognizing kindness, if not practical help, and bade her good night.

*V*espasia meant to consider the puzzling question further when she was alone, but the bed was warm and soft, and she sank almost immediately into a nearly dreamless sleep. When she awoke it was to find Mrs. Naylor herself standing at the foot of the bed with a tray of tea in her hand. She set it on the table and sat down. It was apparent that she had no intention of being dismissed until she was ready to leave. Vespasia might be an earl's daughter, but Mrs.

Naylor was on her own territory, and no one could mistake it.

"Thank you," Vespasia said as calmly as she was able to.

"Drink it," Mrs. Naylor responded. "I've had mine." She poured it and passed the cup to Vespasia. "I have read my daughter's letter. I have no intention of telling either you or Mrs. Alvie what was in it, but I should like you to answer a few questions before I accompany you south to pay my respects at the grave."

Vespasia's response would normally have been anger, but there was both a gravity and a pain in this woman that made anything so self-indulgent seem absurd.

"I will tell you what I can," she said instead, sitting upright in the bed and sipping her tea. She should have felt at a disadvantage, dressed as she was in no more than her nightgown and with her hair around her shoulders, but Mrs. Naylor's candor made that irrelevant also.

"What was your real reason for coming here with Mrs. Alvie?" Mrs. Naylor asked.

Vespasia's ready answer died on her lips. This wild place where life and death hung on a pony's footstep, a few inches between the sure path and the cliff edge or the freezing, squelching bog, stripped one of the pretensions that meant so much in society.

"Then I will tell you," Mrs. Naylor answered for her. "You were afraid she would not make it alone, her courage would fail her, and she would take the many excuses to turn back, if not the first, then the second. Why? What does it matter to you if she fails?"

Vespasia thought for only a moment, then she spoke with absolute certainty. "Omegus Jones spoke of a pilgrimage of expiation, in medieval times," she said. "Then it was so dangerous that often the traveler did not return, but it was an act of supreme friendship for a companion to go with them. It seemed right to me to go, perhaps for my own reasons as well as hers." Only as she said the words did she realize their truth. She had her own expiation to make, for Rome, for dreams she should not have allowed herself to entertain, journeys of the heart she should not have made.

"I see," Mrs. Naylor said. "This Mr. Jones seems to be a remarkable man."

"Yes," Vespasia agreed too quickly, and too sincerely.

Mrs. Naylor smiled. "And that also, I think, has something to do with your reason!"

Vespasia found herself blushing, something she had not done in some time. She was accustomed to being in control—of herself, if not always of the situation.

"Those of us who have lived any of our passions have something to expiate," Mrs. Naylor said gently. "And those who have nothing are the more to be pitied. My father used to say that if you have never made a mistake, then you have probably never made anything at all. Perhaps Mrs. Alvie will realize that in time also. I shall return with you tomorrow, when the ponies have had time to rest and to eat. I have my own journey to make. We shall follow the High Road south, to Tyndrum, and Crianlarich, to Loch Lomond, and from there to Glasgow where we can find a train to London. It will take several days. How many will depend upon the weather, but we should be at Applecross before Christmas." She stood up. "You may do as you please today, but I would suggest that you do not leave the house. You don't know your way, and the Orchy is a hungry river. It reaches out from its banks and claims many lives."

"Mrs. Naylor?"

She turned. "Yes?"

"What is it in this place that holds you?" It was an impertinent question, yet she wished to know so intensely that she defied all the rules of courtesy to ask.

"It is a place of rest on my own journey, Lady Vespasia. Perhaps after I have bidden farewell to my daughter, it may even prove to be the end of it. Why or how is not your concern." She walked to the door, her back ramrod straight, her head high.

Vespasia did not need to be told that the value of Glen Orchy had much to do with Finn, but she was still turning over in her mind the nature of Mrs. Naylor's journey. They had been speaking of the road to answer for mistakes, a nicer word than *sins,* but it held more than the suggestion of mere error. They both knew they were speaking not merely of judgment, but of morality.

She sat in bed sipping her tea and thinking of Kilmuir's terrible death, and the rumors that Isobel had heard, and the gardener's sudden silence at Muir-of-Ord, and most of all of Gwendolen's face when Isobel had suggested obliquely that she could have been attracted to a footman, had he the social position to offer her.

Was Kilmuir really so desperate for children he would have put Gwendolen away by slandering her so completely that society would accept his act, and then marrying Dolly Twyford, leaving Gwendolen an outcast, branded a whore?

Her imagination raced! The possibilities were hideous! She thought of her own children, still little, but one day they would grow up, marry suitably, one hoped with love. What would she do if her daughter faced such ruin of her life? She pictured Kilmuir out driving in the carriage with Mrs. Naylor, the horse taking fright, Kilmuir overbalancing and falling, his wrists caught in the reins. The answer was there in her mind. She would have seized the chance and pushed him and whipped up the horses; at least, she would have thought of it! Whether she would ever have done it she could not know; please God, she would never find out.

Was that what had happened? And Gwendolen had seen it? That was the estrangement between her and her mother. Either she had never realized Kilmuir's plan, or she had refused to believe it. Or perhaps she had willed herself to forget it afterwards, to imagine that somehow he would change his mind, and it would all be all right. He would love her again and deny the rumors. Dolly Twyford would recede into the past. Maybe one day she would even have the longed-for children herself!

And then Mrs. Naylor had ruined it! That would be an estrangement sufficient to send Gwendolen to London, and keep her mother in the farthest reaches of Scotland, farther even than Muir-of-Ord. Perhaps only Glen Orchy would answer that guilt, and maybe even the fear of exposure. Who else might know? Only the staff of the house where it had happened, and they would keep silent, if not from loyalty, then at least for lack of proof. But Mrs. Naylor would no longer wish to live there.

And if she had not done it, would Kilmuir have gone ahead and first slandered Gwendolen and then cast her aside, destitute, and with no home, no friends, no reputation, no skills to earn her own way, except to sell her body on the streets, or more probably, to take her life—as in the end she had done?

Was that what she had heard in Isobel's remark—a beginning of the old accusation again? Was it history repeating itself, and Bertie Rosythe believing just as Kilmuir had pretended to? That might indeed make her despair and embrace death of her own choosing before ruin should overtake her. There was no mother to defend her this time.

How desperately alone she must have felt—a second time falsely accused, and no denial would help. How can one deny something that has only been hinted at, never said? Some people might have attacked in return, but where would that end? Almost certainly in a defeat even more painful. This way ended it almost before it began, certainly before any but a handful of people knew of it.

And then the worst possibility of all struck her. Had Gwendolen believed that Isobel knew Kilmuir's charge and was very subtly telling her so, and threatening a lifelong blackmail, a cat-and-mouse torture never to end? If that was true, no wonder she had killed herself! The thought was hideous beyond the mind to realize. Could it even be true? She hated herself that she could even frame the idea—but Isobel's anger, her need came sharply into focus, as if it had been moments ago that Vespasia had seen the look in her eyes, the desperation for her own social position and safety. Then sanity reasserted itself and she thrust it away. It had been a moment's cruelty, no more.

She rose and dressed at last, weighed down by a sadness and an overwhelming pity for both Gwendolen and Mrs. Naylor. She went downstairs to find breakfast; she knew the wisdom of not attempting anything on an empty stomach, however little she felt like eating.

She found Isobel downstairs, pacing the floor. She turned around the moment she heard Vespasia's footsteps. She looked very pale, dark circles around her eyes making her look ill. "Where have you been?" she demanded.

"I slept late," Vespasia answered. "And I did not get up immediately." That was true as far as it went. She had decided not to tell Isobel of her conversation with Mrs. Naylor, and certainly not of the thoughts that had resulted from it. She was ashamed of where it had led her. She liked Isobel, she always had, but perhaps she did not now trust her as deeply as she once had.

"What are we going to do all day?" Isobel pressed. "What is this place, do you suppose? I have seen all sorts of people here, as if it were a religious retreat."

"Perhaps it is." The thought was not absurd. One could hardly retreat further than this!

Vespasia had a breakfast of oatmeal porridge, then toast and very sharp, pungent marmalade, which, when she inquired, she was told was made on the premises. She immediately purchased two jars to take away with her, regardless of the inconvenience of carrying them. One was for herself, the other for Omegus Jones. She knew his tastes; she had watched him at his own table.

They spent the day quietly. The house proved indeed to be a form of retreat, not religious, but beyond question spiritual. Mrs. Naylor had found a vocation in listening to the troubled, the lonely, and the guilty whose fears robbed them of courage, or the hope that battles could be won.

Vespasia found herself wishing they might stay longer, and she forced herself to remember that this was not her calling, certainly not now, when winter was closing in rapidly. They must accompany Mrs. Naylor to London, and then return to Applecross to report to Omegus and to face Lady Warburton and the others, if they were to still their tongues before spring. They would be bound by the silence of expectation only so long.

She saw Finn several times and observed in him a humor and a great strength of self-understanding, and she perceived without effort why Mrs. Naylor found happiness with him. There was a reserve in him so that there would always be thoughts and dreams to surprise.

It was with regret that she and Isobel set out at daybreak the following morning, with Mrs. Naylor and MacIan, and a troop of ponies. Finn saw them to the entrance of the yard, standing with the fierce wind blowing his hair and whipping at his coat. Vespasia knew his good-byes to Mrs. Naylor had already been said, and words were an encumbrance to the understanding they shared.

They set off south, away from the Glen along the High Road. It was almost seven miles to Tyndrum, and another five or so to Crianlarich. If they pressed on with only such breaks as the horses needed, they might make it by nightfall. On easy roads a carriage would have done it by luncheon, but this was wild country, the peaks snow-covered. They went in the teeth of a gale with ice on its edge, and one good blizzard might end their journey altogether.

But Mrs. Naylor did not hesitate. She led the way with MacIan and left Vespasia and Isobel to keep up the best they could. Their ponies were as good as anyone's; it was a matter of human endurance, and they were half her age. If Mrs. Naylor even thought of doubting them, she gave no sign of it.

They plodded silently through a great sweeping wilderness of mountain and sky, sometimes lit by dazzling sun, blinding off the snow slopes above and ahead. Then squalls would drive down from nowhere, and they huddled together, backs to the worst of it, until it was past and they would plow forward again.

Vespasia glanced at Isobel and received a rueful smile in answer. It was as clear as if they had spoken: At least this flesh-withering cold, the slow, uneven progress, the need to guide their ponies with all possible attention, and even the waste of time to get off and walk, knee-deep in fresh snow, skirts sodden to the thighs, made conversation completely impossible. With Gwendolen's death heavy on heart and mind, it was a blessing, however profound the disguise.

It was well past midday when they reached the inn

at Tyndrum, and the weather was closing in as if it would be all but dark by three.

"We'll no make Crianlarich the night," MacIan said, squinting upward at the sky. "It's after one now, an' it's another five hard miles. We'd best rest the ponies an' start fresh in the morning."

"Surely we can make five miles by dark?" Isobel said urgently. "We've done most of it already!"

"We've done seven, Mistress Alvie," MacIan told her dourly. "Ye mebbe think ye can do the like again, in two hours, but ye're mistaken. An' I'll no have ye drive my ponies to it. Rest while ye can, and be glad of a spot o' warmth." He looked at Mrs. Naylor. "Take a dram, mistress. I'll care for the beasts. Get ye inside."

It was what Vespasia also had dreaded, a long afternoon by the fireside with Isobel and Mrs. Naylor. The meal was endurable. They were all still numb with cold and glad of any food at all, let alone hot, savory haggis rich with herbs, offered them in spite of the nearness to Burns's night. It was served with mashed potatoes and sweet turnips, and afterwards flat, unleavened oatcakes and a delicately flavored cheese covered with oatmeal, called Cabac.

It was finally cleared away, and they were left alone in the small sitting room by the fire, peat to replenish it on the hearth, stags' heads on the wall. The silence was leaden, and Vespasia saw the slight smile cross Mrs. Naylor's lips. She knew in that instant that Mrs.

Naylor understood exactly what was in Isobel's mind, and Vespasia's, and that she was mistress of herself sufficiently to outlast both of them. Grief would wound her, perhaps to the heart, but it would not bend or break her. She would meet them on her own terms.

Twice Isobel began to speak, and then stopped. Finally Mrs. Naylor turned to her.

"Is there something you wish to say, Mrs. Alvie?"

Isobel shook her head. "Only that we cannot sit here in silence all afternoon, but I see that we can, if that is what you wish."

"What would you like to speak about?"

Isobel had no answer.

"Glen Orchy," Vespasia said suddenly. "I should like to know about how you found it, and how word travels of what you do there, and who is welcome."

Mrs. Naylor regarded her with a wry humor, the smile all turned inward, as if facing some moment of decision at last. "You do not ask what I do there, or why I stay," she observed. "Is that because you believe I would not tell you? Or does courtesy suggest it would be intrusive?"

"Both," Vespasia replied. "But principally because I believe that I know."

Isobel looked confused.

Mrs. Naylor ignored her. "Do you indeed?" she said dubiously. "I think not, but we shall not discuss it. If there is debt between us, and I am not sure that there is, then it is you who owe me."

"I have children," Vespasia said gently. She was going to add that she knew the consuming love and need to protect, then she saw the warning in Mrs. Naylor's face, the sudden tightening of fear, and she remembered also that Isobel had been widowed before she had had a chance to bear children. So she said nothing, but she knew that she was right, and Mrs. Naylor knew it also. For the first time, Vespasia took charge of the conversation. She repeated her questions. Mrs. Naylor answered them, and through the darkening afternoon both younger women heard a story of extraordinary courage and strength of will, compassion, and determination, but told in a way that made it seem the most natural and ordinary thing, in fact the only possible way to behave.

Out of an empty house falling into dereliction, Mrs. Naylor and Finn had built and repaired it, until the house was restored to its earlier comfort. Then one guest at a time, first by chance, it had become a hostelry for wanderers who needed shelter not only from the elements of the Highland winter, but from the harder seasons of life, a time to rest and regain not so much strength as a sense of direction, an understanding of mountains, of paths, and above all of hope.

When they retired after dinner Isobel followed Vespasia up the stairs, almost on her heels. "What am I going to do?" she said when they reached the bed-room they were to share. There was a note of desperation in her voice.

"What you have told Omegus that you will do," Vespasia answered. "Mrs. Naylor won't tell people anything other than whatever you tell them yourself."

"I don't mean about Gwendolen's death!" Isobel said impatiently. "I mean about anything! I don't want to marry Bertie Rosythe, even if he offered! Or anyone like him. I should die of loneliness, even if it took me all my life to do it, an inch a day." Her voice was suddenly harsher, as if the anger ran out of control. "For heaven's sake, are you really so damnably complacent that you don't even know what I mean? Can't you see anything further than money and fashion, the season, knowing everyone who matters and having them know you, going to all the right parties?" She flung her hand out stiffly. "When the door is closed, and you take off your tiara and the maid hangs up your gown? Who are you then?" Now she was almost weeping. "What have you? Have you anything at all that matters? Is that what comfort has given you—that you are dead at heart—of self-satisfaction?"

Vespasia saw the contempt in Isobel's eyes and knew that it had been there dormant for all the time they had known each other. Did she care enough to strip away the armor of her own protection to answer truthfully? If not, then she was denying herself, almost as if she were making it true.

"I have too much pain and too much hope to be dead," she replied gravely. "My best days were not wearing a tiara, or a ball gown. I carried bandages, and water, and sometimes even a gun. I wore a plain gray dress that was borrowed, and I stood on the barricades in Rome, and fought for a revolution that failed." She lowered her voice because the tears choked in her throat. "And loved a man I shall never see again. You have no right to despise anyone, Isobel, until at least you know who they are. And we will probably none of us ever know anyone sufficiently well for that. Be happy for it. It is not a sweet thing to look down on others, or to feel their inferiority. It's lonely, ugly, and wrong. Sleep well. We must make Crianlarich, at least, by tomorrow evening. I know it's only about five miles, but five miles of storm in these hills may seem more than thirty miles at home. Good night."

"Good night," Isobel said gently.

The following day they traveled through glancing blizzards, one of them heavy enough to halt them for over two hours, but they reached Crianlarich before sundown, and the day after as far as the head of Loch Lomond, with Ben Lomond towering white in the distance to the south.

After that, they kept close to the water until they were past the Ben itself, and on the morning of the fifth day since leaving Glen Orchy, they bade MacIan good-bye and thanked him heartily. They took the boat to the farthest shore of the loch little more than twenty miles from Glasgow itself. From there it was a matter of hiring a vehicle of any sort and driving their own way to the railway station. With a trap and good roads, even if the weather was inclement, it was a journey that could be done in one day.

After breakfast Isobel was assisted in, then Vespasia, leaving Mrs. Naylor last. Vespasia had intended it so, knowing that Mrs. Naylor was an excellent horsewoman, used to driving. After all, it was she who had gained control of the runaway horse that had killed Kilmuir. Whether it was an accident or not she did not know, nor did she wish to. She herself was a fine rider, but very indifferent at managing a carriage horse, which was a different skill entirely.

Mrs. Naylor hesitated.

Vespasia wondered if memories of Kilmuir's death were returning to her; doubt, guilt, horror, regret— even fear that Gwendolen, having witnessed it from her horse, even a hundred yards away or more, had made her courage for life so fragile. Did she know that her mother had killed to save her? Was that the burden Gwendolen finally could not bear?

Mrs. Naylor sat in the driving seat and picked up the reins awkwardly. She held them in her hands together, not apart in order to give her control of the animal.

The hostler showed her how, patiently, and still she looked clumsy. The horse sensed it and shifted, shaking its head.

The truth struck Vespasia like a hammerblow. Mrs. Naylor did not know how to drive. It was not she who had held the reins when Kilmuir had fallen, accidentally or otherwise; it was Gwendolen herself! Vespasia had seen her in London; she was brilliant at it! And it was Mrs. Naylor who had been out riding and had seen. It made infinitely more sense! She had had to protect her daughter, and Gwendolen, in the shock of it, had allowed herself to forget—to move the blame to a more bearable place.

It fell in front of her eyes in a perfect pattern: The guilt was for having arranged and permitted a marriage to someone like Kilmuir, not to have judged him more accurately. It was a mother's primary duty toward her daughter, and Mrs. Naylor had signally failed. That was why she was prepared to take the burden of guilt now. And Gwendolen had allowed it.

Then in one trivial, cruel remark Gwendolen's fragile new image had been shattered, hope, the shield of forgetting, all gone, and the specter of a lifetime's blackmail from others who knew, or guessed at least part of it.

"I'll drive!" Vespasia said aloud, her voice surprisingly steady. The slight tremor in it could be attributed to the cold. "Let me. I am not as good as Gwendolen was, but I am perfectly adequate." She scrambled forward to take Mrs. Naylor's place. Their eyes met for a moment, and Mrs. Naylor knew that she understood.

Vespasia smiled. It would never be referred to again. Isobel could not afford to—she had her own secrets to keep—and Vespasia had no wish to.

Mrs. Naylor handed her the reins, and they began the last part of their journey to Glasgow, before the long train ride to London.

The journey was tedious, as it had been on the way up, but they reached London at last. It was three days before Christmas. The final meeting was to be at Applecross, and Vespasia knew that Omegus Jones would already be there. There seemed little point in remaining in the city, so she invited Mrs. Naylor and Isobel to go with her to her own country house, which was within ten miles of Applecross. She was uncertain if Mrs. Naylor would wish to accept, and was surprised how it pleased her when she did.

PART THREE

*A*FTER GREETING HER HUSBAND AND CHILDREN, the first thing Vespasia did was to write a letter to Omegus Jones and tell him that they had completed their mission, and it remained only to report that fact to make the oath binding. Then she sealed it and called one of the footmen to ride over and deliver it.

"Shall I wait for an answer, my lady?" he asked.

"Oh, yes! Yes, indeed," she answered him. "It is of the utmost importance!"

"Yes, my lady."

When he returned several hours later and gave her the envelope, she thanked him and tore it open without waiting for him to leave.

My dear Vespasia,

You cannot know how relieved I am to hear that you are safely returned, and that you have accomplished in full all you set out to do. The letter of the law would have sufficed to bind our fellows to silence, but it is the spirit which heals the transgressor, and that is in essence what matters.

I admit I have worried about you, veering from one moment having the utmost faith that you would come to no harm, and the next being plunged into an abyss of fear that some natural disaster might overtake you. Had I known the true extent of your journey to the north, I should not have allowed you to go, and none of this would have succeeded. Perhaps it is good that at times we do not know what lies ahead, or we would not attempt it, and failure would be inevitable.

Naturally, you will wish to be with your own family for Christmas Day, but will you bring Isobel and Mrs. Naylor to Applecross on Christmas Eve, so we may complete our covenant, and Isobel be free?

I await your answer with hope.

Your friend and servant,
Omegus Jones

She folded it with a smile and placed it in her escritoire in the drawer that had a lock on it, then she found Isobel and Mrs. Naylor and gave them Omegus's invitation. The following morning she sent the same footman back with their acceptance.

They set out in the afternoon in order to arrive at Applecross for dinner. The day was crisp and cold, but this far south there was no snow yet, only a taste of frost in the air. By the time they arrived they were shivering, even beneath traveling rugs, and glad to alight and go into the great hall decked with holly and ivy, scarlet ribbons, gold-tipped pinecones, and great bowls of fruit. The fire blazed in the hearth, burning half a log. Footmen met them with glasses of mulled wine and marzipan sweetmeats, warm mince pies and candied peel.

In the hall was a huge fir tree decked with ornaments, candles, and chains of bright-colored paper. Beneath it were small, gaily wrapped gifts. The tree's woody aroma filled the air, along with wood smoke, spiced scents, and, very faintly, the promise of roasted Christmas dinner and hot plum pudding. There was excitement in the whisper of maids' voices and the quick rustle of their skirts.

Omegus was delighted to see them. He complimented Isobel, offered his deepest sympathies to Mrs. Naylor, and said he would tell her all she wished to know when she felt ready to ask, and would take her to the grave at her convenience.

She thanked him and said that festivities of the season must come first. It was a brave and generous thing to do, and exactly what Vespasia would have expected of her.

Ten minutes later when the others had gone, Omegus took Vespasia's arm and held her with a startlingly firm grip when she made to move away. "I think you have more to tell me," he said quietly.

She swiveled to face him. "More?"

He smiled very slightly. "I know you, my dear," he told her. "You would not like Mrs. Naylor, as I see you obviously do, unless you had come to know her more than superficially. You have learned something of her which has moved you to admiration, something you do not give lightly. The same emotion is not in Isobel, so it seems likely to me that you have not confided it in her. I wonder why not, and the answer is possibly to do with Gwendolen's death. Is it something I should know?"

Vespasia found herself blushing. She had not intended to tell him, and now she found she could not lie. It was not that she had not the imagination—it would have been simple enough—but she would lose something she valued intensely were she to place that barrier between them.

In a low, very soft voice, she told him what she had guessed and deduced of the truth of Kilmuir's death.

"And you did not tell Isobel?" he asked gravely.

"No. It . . ." She saw in his eyes the criticism that was unspoken inside herself. "She has a right to know—doesn't she?" she finished.

"Yes." There was no equivocation in him.

"I shall tell her after dinner," she promised. "After she has made peace with Lady Warburton."

His eyebrows rose in question. "Do you not trust

her to keep the same silence for others that she wishes kept for herself?"

Again Vespasia felt the heat burn up her cheeks. "I'm not sure," she confessed. "Mrs. Naylor deserves that silence, and Gwendolen needs it. There is no oath to bind her for that."

He put his hand over hers for an instant, then offered her his arm.

"Shall we go in to dinner?"

The meal was rich and excellent. After the main courses were finished, and long before anyone could think of the ladies withdrawing, Omegus rose to his feet, and the talk ceased.

"My friends, we are met together this Christmas Eve in order to keep an oath that we made less than a month ago. We promised them that if Isobel Alvie were to travel to Scotland and find Gwendolen's mother, Mrs. Naylor, and give her Gwendolen's last letter, and should Mrs. Naylor be willing, accompany her back here, then we would wipe from our memory all knowledge of her remarks to Gwendolen on the night of her death. Her part of that oath has been fulfilled."

"You expect us to take her word for that?" Fenton Twyford asked, his face twisted in sarcasm.

"Mrs. Naylor is here," Omegus answered him. "If you have doubts of Isobel, or of me, then you may ask her." He indicated Mrs. Naylor where she sat calm and dignified at the table.

Fenton Twyford turned to her, met an icy stare, and changed his mind. Then he became aware of his impertinence and blushed.

The flicker of a smile crossed Omegus's face. "It is now up to us to keep our part. Any man or woman who breaks it will cease to be known by the rest of us. We will not speak to them again, invite them to any event public or private, or in any way acknowledge their presence. They will have chosen to be a person whose honor is worthless. I cannot imagine anyone wishes to be such a . . . a creature. Mrs. Naylor has promised to be bound by the same code." He turned to her.

"I have," she said clearly. "And I wish to add to that what Mr. Jones does not know. Mrs. Alvie's part in my daughter's death was smaller than you or she are aware. It was simply the last straw added to a weight Gwendolen was already bearing, placed there by others, of which Mrs. Alvie had only a slight knowledge. I have no intention of telling you what burdens those were. It is better buried with her. Sufficient to say that it would be unjust for Mrs. Alvie to suffer more blame than she has—and which she has washed away by her acts toward me. It is over."

Isobel turned to her, her eyes wide, her lips parted in astonishment and dawning anger. "You mean they were going to punish me—and I was only partly guilty?"

"Yes," Mrs. Naylor agreed.

Isobel swung around to stare at Lady Warburton. "You would have ruined me, driven me into a wilderness from which I would never recover! And I wasn't even guilty! Not entirely . . ."

Lady Warburton quaked. "I didn't know!" she protested. "I thought you were!"

"You thought so yourself!" Blanche Twyford added. "You didn't deny it!"

"Yes, I did!" Isobel spat at her. "You gave no mercy!"

"That is true," Omegus cut across her, his voice clear and insistent, undeniable. "And mercy, the gift to forgive, to wash away from the memory as if it had not happened, to accept the gift of God which is love and hope, courage to begin again in the faith that redemption is come into the world, is the meaning of Christmas. That is why we are met here today. It is why we deck the halls with holly, why the bells will ring tonight from village to village across the land until the earth and the sky are filled with their sound." He turned to Isobel, waiting for her answer, not in words on her lips, but in her eyes.

She hesitated only a moment. "Of course," she answered softly. "I have made my journey and arrived at Christmas, perhaps only at this moment. I shall be grateful all my life that you offered it to me, and to Vespasia for coming with me, when she had no need. How could I accept it for myself, and deny it to another?"

"It is everyone's journey," Omegus said with a smile of utter sweetness. "No man needs to make it alone. But his choice to go with another is the one act of friendship which brings us closest to the Man who was born on the first Christmas, and is the Gift of them all." He raised his glass. "To the friendship which never fades!"

All around the table the answering glasses were lifted.

A CHRISTMAS VISITOR

*T*o those who are willing to give
the best they have

PART ONE

"THERE, MR. RATHBONE, SIR, ARE YER RIGHT?" the old man asked solicitously.

Henry Rathbone tucked the blanket around his legs where he sat in the pony trap, his luggage beside him. "Yes, thank you, Wiggins," he replied gratefully. The wind had a knife-edge to it, even here at the railway station in Penrith. Out on the six-mile road through the snow-crusted mountains down to Ullswater, it would get far worse. It was roughly the middle of December, and exactly the middle of the century.

Wiggins climbed up into the driver's seat and urged the horse forward. It must know its own way by now. It had come here most days when Judah Dreghorn was alive.

But Judah was dead now—and that was Henry's miserable reason for coming back to this wild and marvelous land he loved. Even the place names woke memories of days tramping up long hills, wiry grass under his feet, sweet wind in his face and views that stretched forever. He could see in his mind's eye the pale blue waters of Stickle Tarn looking over toward the summit of Pavey Ark; or the snow-streaked hills of Honister Pass. How many times had he and Judah climbed Scafell Pike to the roof of the world, and sat with their backs to the warm stone, eating bread and cheese and drinking rough red wine as if it had been the food of gods?

Then three days ago he had received a letter from Antonia, her words almost illegible on the paper, to say that Judah had died in a stupid accident. It had not even happened on the lake, or in one of the win-ter storms that raged down the valley with wind and snow, but on the stepping-stones of the stream.

He stared around him now as the pony trap left the town and headed along the winding road westward. The raw, passionate beauty of the land suited his mood. It was steep against an unclouded sky, snow glittering so brilliantly it hurt his eyes, blazing white on the crests, shadowed in the valleys, gullied dark where the rocks and trees broke through.

It was ten years since the four Dreghorn brothers had last been at home together. The family's good for-tune in gaining the estate had meant they could all follow their dreams wherever they led. Benjamin had left his church ministry and gone to Palestine to join in the biblical archaeology there. Ephraim had followed his love of botany to South Africa. His letters were full of sketches of marvelous, unique plants, many of them so useful to man.

Nathaniel, the only other one to marry, had gone to America to study the extraordinary geology of that land, exploring features that Europe did not possess. He had even trekked as far west as the rock formations of the desert territories, and the great San Andreas fault in California. It was there that he had died of fever, leaving his widow, Naomi, to return now in his place.

Antonia had written in her letter that they were all coming home for Christmas, but what a bitter and different arrival that would be. Little wonder Antonia had wanted her godfather to be there. She had terrible news to tell, and no other family to help her. Her parents had died young, she had no siblings; she had only her nine-year-old son, Joshua, who was as bereaved as she.

Henry had known her all her life, first as a grave and happy child, eager to learn, forever reading. She had never tired of asking him questions. They had been friends in discovery.

Then as a young woman a slight self-consciousness in her had put a distance between them. She had shared more reluctantly, but he had still been the first to learn of her love for Judah, and with her parents dead, it was he who had given her away at her wedding.

But what could he possibly do for her now?

Henry tucked the blanket closer around himself and stared ahead. Soon he would see the bright shield of Ullswater ahead, and on a day as clear as this, the mountains beyond: Helvellyn to the south, and the Blencathra range to the north. The high tarns would be iced over, blue in the shadows. Some of the wild animals would have their white winter coats; the red deer would have come down to the valleys. Shepherds would be searching for their lost sheep. He smiled. Sheep survived very well under the snow; their warm breath created a hole to breathe through, and the odor of their sweat made them easy enough to find for any dog worth his keep.

The Dreghorn estate was on the sloping land above the lake edge, a couple of miles from the village. It was the largest for miles, containing rich pasture, woods, streams, and tenant farmhouses, and went right down to the lake shore for more than a mile. The manor house was built of Lakeland stone, three stories high with a south-facing façade.

They went through the gates and pulled up in the driveway. Antonia came out of the front door so soon that she must have been waiting for them, watching at the window. She was tall, with smooth, dark hair, and he remembered her having a unique kind of calm beauty that showed the inner peace that day-to-day irritations could not disturb.

Now as she walked swiftly toward him, her wide,

black skirts almost touching the gravel, her grief was clearly troubled by anger and fear as well. Her skin was pale, tight-stretched across her bones, and her dark eyes were hollowed around with shadows.

He alighted quickly, going toward her.

"Henry! I'm so glad you've come," she said urgently. "I don't know what to do, or how I can face this alone."

He put his arms around her, feeling the stiffness of her shoulders, and kissing her gently on the cheek. "I hope you didn't doubt I would come, my dear," he answered. "And do everything that I can for as long as it may help."

She pulled away and suddenly her eyes filled with tears. She controlled her voice only with the greatest difficulty. "It is so much worse than I wrote. I'm sorry. I don't know what to do to fight it. And I dread telling Benjamin and Ephraim when they arrive. I believe Nathaniel's widow will come, too. You didn't know Naomi, did you?"

"No, I did not meet her." He searched her face, wondering what worse news she could have than Judah's death. What was it she must fight, but had not told him?

She turned away. "Come inside." She gulped on the words. "It's cold out here. Wiggins will bring your things in and put them in your room. Would you like tea, crumpets? It's a little early, but you've come a long way." She was talking too quickly as she led the way up the steps and in through the high, carved front doors. "The fire's hot in the drawing room, and Joshua is still in class. He's brilliant, you know. He's changed a lot since you were last here."

Inside, the hall was warmer, but it was not until they were in the withdrawing room with its red-ochre colored walls and the log fire roaring in the grate that the heat relaxed him a little. He was glad to sit in one of the huge chairs and wait for the maid to bring their tea and toasted crumpets with hot butter.

They were halfway through them before he broke the mood. "I think you had better tell me what else it is that troubles you," he said gently.

She took a deep breath and let it out slowly, then lifted her eyes to meet his. "Ashton Gower is saying that Judah cheated him." Her voice shook. "He says that this whole estate should rightfully have been his, and Judah had him falsely imprisoned, then stole it from him."

Henry felt as if he had been struck physically, so stunned was he by her words. Judah Dreghorn had been a judge in the local court in Penrith, and the most honest man Henry had ever known. The idea of his having cheated anyone was absurd.

"That's ridiculous!" he said quickly. "No one would believe him. You must have your man of affairs warn him that if he repeats such an idiotic and completely false charge, you will sue him."

The shadow of a smile touched her mouth. "I have

already done that. Gower took no notice. He insists
that Judah took the estate after charging him falsely
and imprisoning him, when he knew he was innocent,
all in order to buy the estate cheaply. And of course
that was before the Viking site was found."

He was confused.

"I think you had better tell me the whole story
from the beginning. I don't remember Ashton Gower,
and I know nothing about a Viking site. What happened, Antonia?"

She drank the last of her tea, as if giving herself
time to compose her thoughts. She did not look at
him but into the dancing flames of the fire. Outside it
was already growing dark and the winter sunset lit
the sky and burned orange and gold through the south
windows onto the wall.

"Years ago Ashton Gower's family owned this estate," she began. "It belonged originally to the Colgrave
family, and the widow who inherited it married Geoffrey Gower, and was Ashton's mother. It all seemed
very straightforward to begin with, until Peter Colgrave, a relative from the other side of the family,
raised the question as to whether the deeds were
genuine."

"The deeds to the estate?" Henry asked. "How
could they not be? Presumably Gower's father was
the legal owner, on his marriage to the Colgrave
widow?"

"It was a question of dates," she replied. She

looked tired, drained of all strength. The story was miserably familiar, even if it was also inexplicable. "To do with Mariah Colgrave's marriage and the death of her brother-in-law, and the birth of Peter Colgrave."

"And this Colgrave contested Gower's right to it?" he asked.

She smiled bleakly. "Actually he said the deeds were forged, and that Ashton Gower had done it in order to inherit it himself. He insisted it went to court, so naturally in time it came before Judah, up in Penrith. The first time he examined the deeds he said they looked perfectly good, but he kept them and looked again more closely. He became suspicious and took them to a very good expert on documents in Kendal. He said they were definitely not genuine. He would testify to that."

Henry leaned forward. "And did he?" he asked earnestly.

"Oh, yes. Ashton Gower stood trial for forgery, and was found guilty. Judah sentenced him to eleven years' imprisonment. He has just been released."

"And the estate?" Although he could guess the answer. Perhaps he should have known, but when he had been here before, there had always been better, happier things to talk of—laughter, good food, and good conversation to share.

She shifted a little in her seat.

"Colgrave inherited it," she said ruefully. "But he

did not wish to live here. He put the estate on the market at a very reasonable price. I think actually he had debts to pay. He lived extravagantly. Judah and his brothers all put in what they could, Judah by far the most, and they bought it. He and I lived here. Joshua was born here." Her voice choked with emotion and she needed a few moments to regain control.

He waited without speaking.

"I've never loved a place as I do this!" she said with sudden fierce passion. "For the first time I feel absolutely at home." She gave an impatient little gesture of her hand. "Not the house. It's beautiful, of course, a marvelous house. But I mean the land, the trees, the way the light falls on the water." She searched his face. "Do you remember the long twilight over the lake in the summer, the evening sky? Or the valleys, grassland so green it rolls like deep velvet into the distance, trees full and lush, billowing like fallen clouds? The woods in spring, or the day we followed Striding Edge up toward Helvellyn?"

He did not interrupt her. To remember the beauty that hurt was part of grief.

She was silent for a moment, and then resumed the story. "Of course it's worth a great deal financially as well, even before we found the Viking site. There are the farms, and the houses on the shore. It's easily sufficient to provide for Benjamin, Ephraim, and Nathaniel to follow their own passions." Her face tightened.

"And now that Nathaniel's dead, for Naomi, of course."

"What is this Viking site you keep referring to?" he asked.

She smiled. "A shepherd from one of the farms found a silver coin and he brought it to Judah. Judah was always interested in coins, and he knew what it was." She smiled. "I remember how pleased he was, because it was rather romantic, it was Anglo-Saxon, Alfred the Great, who defeated the Danes, or at least held them at bay, in the late 800s. The coin we found might have been part of the Danelaw tribute, since the rest of it was Viking silver, ornaments, jewelry, and harness. When we found the whole treasure there were Norse Irish brooches, and arm rings, Scandinavian neck rings, Carolingian buckles from France, and coins from all over, even Islamic ones from Spain, North Africa, the Middle East, and as far as Afghanistan." Her wonder stayed for a moment or two longer, then faded as the present intruded again.

"Judah invited professional archaeologists in, of course," she resumed. "And they dug very carefully. It took them all of one summer, but they uncovered the ruins of a building, and in it the whole hoard of coins and artifacts. Most of the things are in a museum, but lots of people come to see the ones we kept, and naturally they stay in the village. Our lakeside cottages are let nearly all the time."

"I see."

She turned to look at him directly. "We had no idea it was there when we bought the estate! No one did. And the whole village profits from the visitors."

"Is Gower suggesting that you did know about the hoard?" he asked.

"Not in so many words, but he is allowing it to be understood."

"What exactly is he saying?" He could not help her to fight it if he did not know the truth, however ugly or distressing. The thought of Judah, of all men, being accused of dishonesty was most painful.

"That the deeds to the estate were genuine," she replied. "And that Judah knew it all along, and bribed the expert to lie, so Colgrave could inherit, sell the property quickly and cheaply, because he needed the money, and Judah could buy it, and then pretend to discover the hoard."

Henry saw at a glance both that the charge was preposterous, and that it could also be extremely difficult to disprove because it rested on no reasonable evidence. Gower was obviously a bitter man who had been punished for a particularly stupid crime, and now lashed out seeking some kind of vengeance, rather than trying to salvage and rebuild his life.

"Surely no one believed him," he said aloud. "The expert said the deeds were forged, and there is nothing to suggest anyone at all knew of the Viking site. After all, it must have been there for centuries. None of Gower's ancestors knew of it, did they?"

"No! No one had the faintest idea," she agreed.

"Chance," he replied.

"I know that. But Gower is saying that we only waited long enough to make it seem as if we didn't know. But it alters nothing, if the deeds were genuine. It is only a small lie on top of a greater one." Her voice dropped a little. The fire was burning lower and the lamplight softened the misery in her face. "Can you think of anything worse than to send an innocent man to prison, and blacken his reputation in order to steal his inheritance? That is what he is saying Judah did. And now he is not even here to defend himself!" She was close to losing control. The careful mask, which cost her so much, was beginning to slip.

Henry felt the need to say something quickly, but it must be both helpful and true. False comfort now would only make things worse later, and though she might well understand why he had done it, she would never trust him again.

"He made these charges before Judah's death?" he asked. The truth was a poor refuge, but it was all he had.

She looked up at him.

"Yes. He came out of prison in Carlisle, straight back here." Suddenly anger took hold of her. "Why couldn't he have gone somewhere else, and started a new life where he wasn't known? If he'd gone to Liverpool or Newcastle, no one would have known he'd been in prison, and he could have begun again! I've never seen anyone so filled with anger. I've seen him in the street, and he frightens me." She looked terrified. Her magnificent eyes were wide and hollow, her face almost bloodless.

"Surely you don't think he would hurt you?" he exclaimed. The lights were exactly as before, and the coals were still hot, but it was as if the room were darker. "Antonia?"

She turned away from him. "No," she said quietly. "You're really asking if he hurt Judah, aren't you?" She drew in a long breath. "We'd been into the village for a violin recital. It was a wonderful evening. We took Joshua, even though it was late, because we knew he'd love it. He is going to be one of the world's great musicians. He has already composed simple pieces, but beautiful, full of unusual cadences. He took one of them, and the violinist played it. He asked if he could keep the copy." Her face filled with pride at the memory.

"Perhaps he will be England's Mozart," he answered.

She said nothing for a few moments, struggling to regain her composure.

"Perhaps," she agreed at last. "When we came home it was after ten o'clock. I saw Joshua to bed. He was so excited he wanted to stay up all night. Judah said he wanted to walk. He had been sitting all evening. He . . . never came back." Again she took a few moments before she could continue. "A while after, I woke Mrs. Hardcastle, and we sent for Wiggins. He and the butler and the footman went out with lanterns to look for Judah. It was the longest night of my life. It was after three when they came back and said they had found him in the stream. He had apparently tried to cross in the dark over the stepping-stones and slipped. They are very smooth there, and could be icy. There is a slight fall a few yards down where they are jagged. They believe he slipped and struck his head, and the water carried him."

"Where to? It's not very deep." Was he thinking of the right place, remembering accurately?

"No, but it doesn't have to be to drown. If he had been conscious he would naturally have climbed out. He might have caught pneumonia from the cold, but he would be alive." She took a deep breath. "Now I must fight the slander for him." She lifted her eyes to meet his. "It is hard enough to lose him, but to hear Ashton Gower say such evil things of him, and fear that anyone at all could believe it, is more than I can bear. Please help me prove that it is absolutely and terribly wrong. For Judah's sake, and for Joshua."

"Of course," he said without hesitation. "How can you doubt that I would?"

She smiled at him. "I didn't. Thank you."

*S*upper was early, and there were only the three of them at the table. Henry did not sit at the head, in Judah's place. It seemed an insensitive thing to do, not only for Antonia, but for the grave, pale-faced Joshua, who had not yet reached his tenth birthday, and was so suddenly bereft of his father.

Henry did not know him well. Last time he had been here Joshua had been only five, and spent more time in the nursery. Already he had played the piano and had been too fascinated by it to pay much attention to a middle-aged gentleman here for a week in the summer, and more interested in hill walking than music lessons.

Now he sat solemn-eyed, eating his food because he had been told to, and staring at the space on the wall opposite his seat, somewhere between the Dutch painting of cows in a quiet field, and an equally flat seascape of the Romney Marshes with light glistening on the water as if it were polished pewter.

The servants came and went with each dish, soundless and discreet.

Henry tried speaking to Joshua once or twice, and received a considered answer each time. Henry had a son, but Oliver was a grown man, one of London's most distinguished barristers, well known for his brilliance in the criminal court. Henry could hardly remember now what Oliver had been like at nine years old. He too had been intelligent, certainly, precocious in his ability to read, and as far as Henry could remember, in his taste in books. He had been inquisitive, and profoundly argumentative. He could recall that clearly enough! But that was nearly thirty years ago, and the rest was hazy.

He wanted to speak to Joshua, so as not to appear to ignore him.

"Your mother says you composed a piece of music that the violinist at the recital played," he observed. "That is very fine."

Joshua regarded him soberly. He was a handsome child with wide, dark eyes like Antonia's, but his father's brow and balance of head.

"It did not sound exactly how I meant it to," he replied. "I shall have to work harder at it. I think it ends a little soon . . . and it's too quick."

"I see. Well, knowing what is wrong with a thing is at least halfway toward putting it right," Henry replied.

"Do you like music?" Joshua asked.

"Yes, very much. I can play the piano a little." Actually, he was being quite modest. He had a certain flair for it. "But I cannot write for it."

"What can you do?"

"Joshua!" Antonia remonstrated.

"It's quite all right," Henry said quickly. "It is a

160

fair question." He turned to the boy. "I am good at mathematics, and I like to invent things."

"You mean arithmetic?"

"Yes. And algebra and geometry."

Joshua frowned. "Do you like it, or is it that you have to do it?"

"I like it," Henry replied. "It makes a very beautiful kind of sense."

"Like music?"

"Yes, very much."

"I see."

And then the conversation rested, apparently to Joshua's satisfaction.

After a postprandial half hour by the fire, Henry excused himself, saying that he wanted to take a walk and stretch his legs. He did not ask Antonia where Judah had died, but when he had his coat and boots on, and a hat and scarf as well, he inquired from Wiggins, and was given directions to the stream nearly a mile away.

It was nearly half past eight, and outside the night was dense black, apart from the lantern he was holding, and the few lights he could see from the village a couple of miles away. The sound of his feet on the gravel was loud in the cloaking silence.

He moved very slowly, uncertain of his way, wary of tripping over the edge of the lawn, or even of bumping into the drive gates. It took a few minutes for his eyes to become sufficiently accustomed to see ahead of him by starlight, and make out the black tracery of bare branches against the sky. Even then it was more by the blocking of the pinpricks of light than the line of a tree. A sickle moon made little difference, just a silver curve like a horn.

Why on earth had Judah Dreghorn walked so far late on a night like this? The cold stung the skin. The wind was from the north, off the snows of Blencathra. Here in the valley the ground was frozen like rock, but there was no gleaming whiteness to reflect back the faint light. He wound his scarf more tightly around his neck and a trifle higher about his ears, and moved forward on what he hoped was the way Wiggins had told him.

Judah had not simply gone for a walk. Henry felt it was stupid to persist in believing that. The recital had been splendid, a triumph for Joshua. Why would a man leave his wife and son after such an event, and go feeling each footstep over the frozen ground in the pitch dark?

Except, of course, it was more than a week ago now, so the moon would have been almost half full and there would have been more light. Still, it was a strange thing to go out at all, even with a full moon, and why so far?

Judah had gone to the stream, and tried to cross over it. So he had intended going even farther. To where? Henry should have asked Antonia where the Viking site was. But why would Judah go there at night? To meet someone urgently, or with whom he did not wish to be seen.

Henry was following some sort of path. If he kept the lantern out in front of him, he could walk at about normal speed. It was bitterly cold. He was glad for gloves, but even with them his fingers were stiff.

Who would Judah meet secretly, beyond the stream, at that time of night? The answer that leaped to the mind was Ashton Gower. If it had been any other man, Henry might have thought he was looking for some accommodation, a bargain regarding the trial and the deeds, and Gower's subsequent accusation, but Judah had never equivocated with the truth.

If, on the other hand, he had taken pity on Gower in any way, he would have done it openly, before lawyers and notaries. If he made any threat, that too would have been plain and open.

Perhaps it had not been Gower, but someone else. Who? And why? No believable answer came to his mind.

The land was rising and he leaned forward into the wind. Its coldness stung his skin. He could hear the stream rattling over the stones, and somewhere in the distance a dog fox barked, an eerie sound that startled him so he nearly dropped the light.

He moved slowly now, lifting the lantern so it shed its glow farther. Even so, he nearly missed the path to the stones. The water was running quite rapidly, oily black breaking pale where the surface was cut by jagged lumps poking through, sharp-edged. Then he realized it was the fall he was looking at. The stepping-stones were upstream about thirty yards, smooth, almost flat.

But when he reached them and looked more closely, he saw the rime of ice where the bitter air had frozen them moments after the current had washed over. What on earth had Judah been thinking of to try standing on them? What had absorbed his mind so intently that he had taken such a risk?

Puzzled and weighed down by sadness, he turned and made his way back toward the house.

*I*n the morning he was woken by the housekeeper, Mrs. Hardcastle. She was smiling and carrying a tray of tea. He sat up, startled to see daylight outside. That must mean it was nearer nine o'clock than eight.

"And why not?" she asked reasonably when he protested that she should not have let him lie in. "It was a long way you came yesterday. All the way up from London!" She set the tray down, poured the tea for him, then went and drew open the curtains. "Not so nice today," she said briskly. "You'll be wanting all your woolies on, likely. Wind's off the water, and there's snow on it for sure. Take the skin off your face, it will, if it blows up proper." She turned back to him. "Mrs. Dreghorn said to tell you as Mr. Benjamin's coming today. Telegraph says he'll be in Penrith by noon, so we'll be going to fetch him, as long as the weather holds off. If not, he'll be having to stay at the inn there, which would be a shame, since he's come a fair distance, too."

Mrs. Hardcastle could have little idea of the reality if she could liken a train journey from London to rail and ship and whatever else it had taken for Benjamin Dreghorn to come from Palestine to the Lakes in the middle of winter. But Henry forbore from saying so, since very probably she did little more than read and write. Geography may not have been among her needs.

"Indeed," he said, sipping his tea. "Let us hope the weather favors us."

But it did not. By half past ten when Henry set out in the trap with Wiggins, clouds were piling up in the north and west over the Blencathra Mountains, shadowing the land and promising more snow. Wiggins shook his head and pursed his lips, and added more blankets for his passengers.

They were at least halfway to Penrith before the sky darkened and the wind rose with a knife-edge to it, and the first white flurries came. Henry had not seen Benjamin Dreghorn for several years and normally would have looked forward to meeting him again, but this time it would be very hard. He had offered to go, in order to save Antonia having to be the one to break the news. Naturally, when Benjamin had set out from Palestine several weeks ago, there had been nothing but happiness in view. The bitterness of his arrival would be totally unexpected.

Henry huddled with the blanket around him and the driving snow at his back as they went the last few miles. He hoped the train had not been delayed. If the snow was bad over Shap Fell, it could hold them up. They would simply have to wait for it. He twisted around in his seat, staring behind him, but all he could see was gray-white, whirling snow; even the closer hills and slopes were obliterated.

Wiggins hunched his shoulders, his hat over his ears. The pony trudged patiently onward. Henry tried to arrange his thoughts so he could tell Benjamin as gently as possible.

The train was no more than twenty minutes after the hour. The snow was beginning to drift in places, but the wind had driven it on the lee side at Shap, and the line was not badly affected.

Henry stood on the platform and watched the carriage doors open and searched for Benjamin's tall figure among the dozen or so people who got off. He was the last to come, carrying two largish cases and smiling broadly.

Henry felt his chest tighten as he forced himself to walk toward Judah's brother.

"Henry Rathbone!" Benjamin said with unaffected

delight. He put the cases down carefully on the snowy platform and held out his hand.

Henry took it, wrung it, then reached for one of the cases to help.

"It's good to see you!" Benjamin said enthusiastically. "Are you staying for Christmas?" He picked up the other case. "What filthy weather! But by heaven, it's beautiful, isn't it? I'd forgotten how incredibly clean it is, after the desert. And water everywhere." He strode forward and Henry had to make an effort to keep up with him. "I used to hate the rain," Benjamin went on. "Now I appreciate that water is life. You get to value it in Palestine. I can't begin to tell you how exciting it is to walk where Christ walked."

A blast of icy wind struck them as they turned the corner into the street, and took a few minutes to exchange greetings with Wiggins, load the luggage, and make their way out of the town and onto the road west again.

Benjamin resumed his tale. "You wouldn't believe the places I've been to, Henry. I've stood by the shores of Galilee, probably the very hill on which Christ preached the Sermon on the Mount. Can you imagine that? I've been to Capernaum, Caesarea, Bethlehem, Tarsus, Damascus, but above all, I've walked the streets of Jerusalem and out toward Golgotha. I've stood in the Garden of Gethsemane!" His voice rang with the wonder of it. Even muffled against the wind and snow his sunburned face glowed.

"You are very fortunate," Henry replied, meaning it, in spite of how irrelevant it seemed now. "Not only to see it, but to be so aware of its meaning."

"I've brought something very special as a Christmas present for Joshua," Benjamin went on. "I'm not sure if he'll like it, yet, but he will in time. I've got it in the brown case, that's why I've been so careful with it. Antonia will keep it for him, if necessary. But he must be nine by now. I think he'll understand."

"What is it?"

Benjamin smiled broadly. He was a handsome man, strong-boned, and he had excellent teeth. "A piece of manuscript—an original of half a dozen verses from the New Testament, just a page, but can you imagine how the man who wrote it must have felt?" His voice rang with enthusiasm. "It's in a carved, wooden box. Beautiful work. And it smells marvelous. They told me it was the odor of frankincense."

"I am sure he will like it," Henry responded. "If not just yet, then in a year or two."

"Wait until Judah sees it," Benjamin said eagerly.

Henry could leave it no longer. Not to speak now would amount to a lie. He turned sideways, the wind making his eyes water.

"Benjamin," he began. "I came to meet you personally, not only because I am pleased to see you, but because I have some very hard news which I wanted to spare Antonia from having to tell you herself . . ."

The light and the joy drained out of Benjamin's

face. Suddenly his blue eyes were bleak and the biting cold of the snow and the wild, color-bleached landscape seemed hostile, the chill of it getting into the bones.

Henry did not wait. "Judah died in an accident eight days ago. He went out at night and slipped on the ice of the stepping-stones crossing the stream."

Benjamin stared at him. "Died! He couldn't have—it's only a couple of feet deep at the most, if that!" he protested.

"He must have hit his head on the stones." Henry did not go into any more detail. The explanation made no difference to the truth of it.

"What was he doing there at night?" Benjamin demanded. "There's nothing there!"

"No one knows," Henry replied. "He just said he wanted to stretch his legs before going to bed. He had taken Antonia and Joshua to a recital in the village."

"It doesn't make sense!"

Henry did not argue. He knew better than to say that such unexpected tragedy seldom did.

Benjamin turned forward and stared into the snowstorm, his face immobile, marked with uncomprehending grief. How could the whole world change in an instant, and with no warning?

They rode for at least another mile without speaking again, and were rounding the last curve in the road when the snow eased and a blue patch appeared in the sky. A bar of light like silver shone on the flat surface of the lake, so brilliant it dazzled the eyes. The village itself was almost invisible with its white-blanketed roofs.

If Henry were to tell Benjamin about the accusation, and save Antonia from having to do it, then he had little time left.

"Benjamin, that is not all I have to tell you before we reach the house," he said aloud. "I would prefer that Antonia, who told me, did not have to go through it all again."

Benjamin turned slowly. "Judah's dead. What else can there be?" His face was full of pain. He had loved his brother profoundly, and his admiration for him had been intense. The only thing worse than having to tell him of Gower's accusation would be having him find out from someone else.

"Ashton Gower is saying that Judah imprisoned him wrongly, in order to be able to buy the estate," Henry said simply. "It is nonsense, of course, but we need to find a way to force him to retract it, and never repeat it again. It is causing much distress."

"Ashton Gower is in prison, where he belongs," Benjamin replied a trifle coldly. "Exactly who is it that is spreading these lies? I'll put a stop to it, by law, if necessary." He spoke forcefully. He was a powerful man, as were all the Dreghorn brothers, but he had a remarkable intellect as well. He had succeeded brilliantly at university and it was something of a surprise to his family when he had chosen to study theology. But then when his income from the estate had freed him from the need to earn his way, and he had followed his scholastic dreams to the Holy Land, everyone had found it quite natural.

"Gower has served his sentence," Henry corrected him. "He is free, and unfortunately has chosen to come back to the Lakes."

"When?"

"About a month ago."

"Then I'll go and see him myself. I'm surprised he hasn't been run out of the village. What kind of a man slanders the dead, and adds to the bereavement of a widow and her child? He's less than filth!"

"He is a deeply unpleasant man . . ." Henry began.

"He is a convicted forger and a would-be thief!" Benjamin retorted. "If it hadn't been for Colgrave he'd have got away with it."

"But he made his accusations when Judah was still alive," Henry finished. "I don't believe he has repeated them publicly since then, but no doubt he will. He is determined to clear his own name."

Benjamin gave a bark of laughter and his face set hard and angry.

There was no more time for conversation. They approached the gates of the estate and Henry climbed down to open them, then close them after the trap. He walked behind them up the gravel to the door just as Antonia came out.

Benjamin leaped out of the trap and strode the couple of paces over to her and took her in his arms, holding her gently as if she were a hurt child.

Then he looked up and saw Joshua standing in the front doorway, dwarfed by the massive lintels and looking embarrassed and unhappy.

Benjamin let go of Antonia and walked up the step. For an instant he seemed uncertain how to treat Joshua. He hesitated, torn between taking him in his arms or grasping him by the hand.

Joshua gulped, standing perfectly still. "Hello, Uncle Benjamin," he said very quietly.

Benjamin knelt down. "Hello, Joshua." He held out his arms, and the child allowed himself to be embraced, then after a long moment, very slowly returned it, sliding his arms around Benjamin's neck and laying his head on his shoulder.

Henry found himself overcome with emotion also, and turned away to Antonia. He offered her his arm up the steps, and Wiggins followed with Benjamin's cases.

The following morning Henry got up early because he did not want to lie in bed thinking. When he reached the dining room he found Benjamin already there, with a plate of Cumberland sausage, eggs and bacon, and thick, brown toast on the side. Instead of marmalade there was a dark, rich jam in the dish. He remembered from the past that it was witherslacks, a tart kind of small plum, known as a damson in the rest of England, and Benjamin's favorite.

Benjamin gave him a tight, miserable smile. "Good morning, Henry. I'm going to see Colgrave this morning. It must have snowed most of the night. It's pretty deep. We can ride. It's only a couple of miles or so. He's an oily swine, and if he had an ounce of decency he'd have stopped Gower already, but we might be able to put a little backbone into him." He took another mouthful from his plate. "Or make him more frightened of us than of whatever he thinks Gower will do to him. Ephraim should be here any day, but you can't tell how long it will take to sail from South Africa. What a terrible homecoming!"

"Antonia is expecting Naomi, too," Henry told him.

"I doubt she can help." Benjamin's broad shoulders slumped. "I still miss Nathaniel. What's happening to us, Henry? Judah was the oldest, and he was only forty-three, and two of us are dead already! Joshua's the only heir to the Dreghorns."

"So far," Henry agreed.

Benjamin did not answer the remark. "Have some breakfast," he said instead. "You can't go out in this weather without a good meal inside you."

And in spite of the fact that it was only just over a

mile and a half to Peter Colgrave's house, it was not an easy journey. The snow had drifted in the night and in places it was more than two feet deep.

They rode toward the lake and crossed the stream lower down where there was a rough bridge made of two long slabs of stone balanced at either end, and on a central stone. On foot, one balanced with care, but on horseback it was a matter of splashing through, more than hock-deep, and up the other side.

Half a mile beyond they saw the square-towered stone church and the vicarage, then a hundred yards farther was Colgrave's house, also of stone. It was handsome, deep-windowed, the roof immaculately slated. One could see where the money from the sale of the estate had been used to remain and extend it, and to build new stables. That was where they left their horses.

"Come in," Colgrave said, covering his surprise and considerable reluctance with an effort. "Good to see you, Dreghorn. My deepest condolences on your brother's death. Terrible tragedy."

"Thank you," Benjamin said briefly. "You remember Henry Rathbone, don't you?"

"Can't say that I do," Colgrave answered, looking Henry up and down, trying to place his lean figure and mild, aquiline face. "How do you do, Mr. Rathbone."

Henry replied, finding it difficult to smile. Colgrave was broad, tending to fat a little, although he was no more than forty at the most. He had dark brown hair and a clever, thoughtful face, somewhat guarded in expression.

"Come in, gentlemen," Colgrave invited, ushering them through a wood-paneled hall decorated with fine portraits of men and women who were presumably his ancestors. The fire was already burning well in his study and the room was warm. The shelves that lined the walls were stocked with leather-bound, gold-lettered books. "What may I do for you?" Colgrave asked. "Anything I can, to be of assistance. You will be returning to the east? Palestine, isn't it? Must be fascinating." This was directed to Benjamin. He considered Henry to be of no importance, merely a friend brought for company, and perhaps that was close enough to the truth.

"Not until I have cleared my brother's name," Benjamin said bluntly.

"Oh!" Colgrave let out his breath. "Yes. Fearful business." His face tightened in distaste. "Gower is a complete outsider, quite appalling. The man is a fraud, a cheat, and now slanders the name of a good man. Pity we can't set the dogs on him." He gave a slight shrug of his heavy shoulders.

"If it were as simple as that, I should not need your help," Benjamin retorted. "You saw the original deeds that he is saying were genuine."

Colgrave raised his eyebrows.

"Of course. They were so badly forged I don't

know how anyone believed them for a moment, except that I suppose many of us are not familiar with such papers, and we are not in the habit of suspecting our neighbors of such a stupid crime."

"But you would swear that they were forged?" Benjamin pressed.

"My dear fellow, I did! In court. Not that it rested on my testimony alone, of course. There was an expert from Kendal, came and also swore they were complete forgeries from beginning to end. We all knew that." He waved his hand. "This will blow over, you know. No one with any sense at all believes Gower. The only ones who ever listen to him are newcomers. There are half a dozen families, one or two with money, I admit, who weren't here at the time, so they don't understand."

"Who are they?" Benjamin asked.

"Leave it alone for a while," Colgrave said soothingly. "I'll speak to them on your behalf, and tell them the truth of the thing. Go now, in hot blood, and you'll only make enemies of them. No one likes to be shown up for a fool, you know?"

"A fool?" Benjamin asked.

"Certainly, a fool. Who but a fool would believe a convicted forger like Ashton Gower? They'll learn the truth of him soon enough. Wait until he loses that foul temper of his with them! Or borrows a horse and brings it home lame, as he did with poor Bennion, or tries to borrow money we all know he'll never return. Then they'll wish they'd had more sense than to give him a moment's credence. As angry as you are, quite rightly, of course, you'll make enemies of them now."

Henry disliked having to agree with Colgrave, but honesty gave him no choice. They excused themselves and left, but as soon as they were outside Benjamin turned around.

"Before we get the horses, I want to go to the churchyard." He took a deep breath, his face bleak and half turned away. "I must see Judah's grave."

"Of course," Henry agreed. "So must I. Or would you rather be alone?"

Benjamin hesitated.

"I'll wait," Henry said quickly. "I can go later. I'll fetch the horses, then we don't have to go back."

Benjamin nodded, unwilling to commit himself to speech, but his gratitude was in his eyes.

Henry stood still for a moment or two, watching him walk slowly, crunching through the snow, until he reached the stone wall of the churchyard, and then was lost behind the yew branches.

He went back to the stable yard, and by the time he returned, Benjamin was waiting for him.

"I want to see Leighton, if he's still the doctor here," he said, taking his horse from Henry and mounting. "If not him, then whoever is. I don't know how Judah could have been stupid enough to slip on the stepping-stones. He's lived here all his life. Where was he going, anyway? What was he doing crossing the stream alone at that time of night? Why did he go out at all?"

"I don't know," Henry admitted, keeping the horses in step, side by side as they rode toward the village. "Are you sure it matters now?"

Benjamin looked at him sharply. "Of course it matters! It doesn't make any sense. There's something wrong, and I intend to get to the truth. Ashton Gower has to be silenced, and permanently. We can't let Antonia live in fear that he'll start up again." He was angry with Henry for not understanding; it was clear in his face and the tone of his voice.

Grief and confusion were wounding him and Henry understood that. Still the response stung, and it was an effort to control his own reaction. He had liked Benjamin all the years he had known him, as much as he had liked Judah, and the sense of loss incurred was no stranger to him. It was many years since his wife had died, but the memory was still there.

It was still snowing very lightly but the wind had dropped. Fifteen minutes later they were at the doctor's house and the horses by the gate. It was another quarter of an hour before he was free to see them.

"Terribly sorry," Leighton said to Benjamin. "Dreadful thing to happen. Good of you to come up, Rathbone. What can I do for you?" He was a thin man, full of nervous energy but with a grave voice, nearer Henry's age than Benjamin's.

Benjamin's face was slightly flushed, as much from helpless anger as the sharp edge of the cold outside. "There's a lot about Judah's death that makes no sense," he replied. "I wanted to find the truth of what happened." He stood in the middle of the room, lean, broad-shouldered, skin burned brown by the sun of the Holy Land, his face hard.

Leighton had been a country doctor for twenty years. He understood grief and the anger that prompted men to fight it. He leaned against the bookcase and regarded Benjamin seriously. "The facts are simple. Judah went out for a walk at about half past ten in the evening. There was a half moon, but it was still extremely dark. He took a lantern, which was found washed up on the banks of the stream a few yards from where he was. When he did not return home, some little while after midnight, Antonia became sufficiently alarmed to send out the male servants to search for him. They found his body caught in the rocks of the fall a short distance below the stepping-stones."

"I know all that!" Benjamin said impatiently. "Henry told me. What was he doing there? Why did he go out at all? Why did he try crossing icy stepping-stones at night? Where was he going? How does a strong man drown in two feet of water? The stream isn't running fast enough to sweep anyone off their feet, even at this time of the year. I've fallen off those stepping-stones a dozen times, and got no worse than wet clothes!"

"You can fall off a horse a hundred times and get no worse than bruises, or a broken collarbone," Leighton said reasonably. "But the hundred and first fall can kill you. Benjamin, don't look for reasons where there are none. He slipped in the dark and fell badly. He struck his head on the stones and it knocked him senseless. If it hadn't, no doubt he'd have climbed out and walked home again. Tragically, it did."

"How do you know he struck his head when he fell?" Benjamin challenged. "How do you know no one struck him?"

Leighton's face darkened. "Don't start thinking like that, Benjamin," he warned. "There's no evidence to suggest anything of the sort. Judah slipped. It was a tragic accident. He drowned. The stream carried him down to the fall, and . . ."

"You examined him?" Benjamin interrupted.

"Of course I did."

"What did you find, exactly?"

Leighton sighed. "That the cause of death was drowning. There were several abrasions on his head and shoulders, one where a smooth stone had struck him, which would be when he fell, several others rougher, where the current carried him down onto the fall."

"Are you sure it was those stones?" Benjamin persisted.

"Yes. The wounds had little bits of riverweed in them, and his hands were scraped by the gravel at the bottom." His face was sad and patient. "Benjamin, there's nothing more to it than I've told you. Don't look for reasons or fairness in it. There aren't any. It is an unjust tragedy, the death of a good man who should have lived a long and happy life. These things happen, probably more often than you know, because it doesn't hit you like this unless it was someone you loved. People die on the mountains, there are boating accidents on the lakes, falls in the hunting field. I'm sorry."

"But why was he out crossing the stream in the middle of the night?" Benjamin could not let it go.

Leighton frowned. "Nobody knows that. I don't suppose we ever will. Look to what matters now. Help Antonia to come to terms with it. Be a support to her, and do what you can for young Joshua. They need your strength now, not a lot of questions to which we'll find no answers. And even if we found them all, they would make no difference to what happened. Make the best of what is left."

Benjamin looked bewildered. "And Ashton Gower?" he demanded angrily. "Who is going to silence him? I swear by God, if he goes on blackening Judah's name, I will! And if he had anything to do with Judah's death, anything at all, I'll prove it and I'll see him hang!"

Leighton's face was grim. He straightened up, frowning. "You can be forgiven a certain amount for the shock of your loss, Benjamin, but if you suggest, outside this room, that Gower had anything to do with your brother's death, you will be even more guilty of slander than he is. There is nothing whatever to indicate that he met Judah or had any intention of harming him, then or at any time. Please don't bring any more grief on your family than it already has. It would be utterly irresponsible."

Benjamin stood without moving for a long moment, then turned and strode out, leaving the door swinging behind him.

"I'm sorry," Henry apologized for him. "Judah's death has hit him very hard, and Ashton Gower's charges are vicious and profoundly wrong. Judah was one of the most honest men I ever knew. To blacken his name now is an evil thing to do. I agree with Benjamin completely, and regardless of what he does, I will do all I can to protect Judah's widow and son from such calumny."

"Everyone in the village will," Leighton said gravely. "Gower is a deeply unpopular man. We all remember what he did over the forged deeds. He's arrogant and abrupt. But if Benjamin accuses him over Judah's death, he will make it a great deal more difficult than it has to be, because some are then going to see injury on both sides, and it will become a feud, and split the village. That kind of thing can take years to heal, sometimes generations, because people get so entrenched, other grievances are added, and they can't turn back."

"I'll speak to him," Henry promised. Then he excused himself and went outside into the snow to catch up with Benjamin.

Benjamin was standing holding both the horses. He looked at Henry defiantly, his blue eyes burning. "I know," he said before Henry could speak. "I just hate being told by that satisfied, self-righteous . . ." He stopped. "It's thirsty work walking in this. Let's go to the Fleece and take a pint of Cumberland ale. It's a long time since I've tasted a jar of Snecklifter. It's too early for lunch, or I'd have had a good crust of bread and a piece of Whillimoor Wang. There's a plain, lean cheese for you to let you know you're home. I'd like to hear a tale or two of good men and dogs, or even a fanciful yarn of demons and fairies, such as they like around here. They used to write that in as cause of death sometimes, you know? Taken by fairies!"

Henry smiled. "That must have covered a multitude of things!"

Benjamin laughed harshly. "Try explaining that to the constable."

An hour later, warmed and refreshed, entertained by taller and taller stories in broad Cumberland dialect, they emerged into the street again to find the weather brighter, and the sun breaking through wide rifts in the clouds, dazzling on the snow and reflecting on the lake in long blue and silver shards.

They had ridden barely a hundred yards, past small shops, the smithy, the cooper's yard, and were just level with the clog shop where the clog maker was hollowing out the wooden soles with his long, hinged stock knife when they almost ran into a broad-shouldered man with densely black hair.

The man was on foot and Benjamin looked down at him with an expression of cold fury. The man's eyes were narrowed, hard with loathing as he stared back. Henry did not need to be told that this was Ashton Gower.

"So you've returned from following the footsteps of God!" Gower said sarcastically. "Much good it'll do you. I'll give you a decency of mourning, for the widow's sake, though those that profit from sin are as guilty of it as them that do it. But I suppose a woman's got to stay by her man, she's little choice. It'll make no difference in the end."

"None at all," Benjamin agreed harshly. "Speak another word against my brother, and I'll sue you for slander and see you back in prison, which is where you belong. They should never have let you out."

"Slander's a civil suit, Mr. Dreghorn," Gower replied, glaring up at him. "And you'd have to win before you could do anything to anyone. I've no money to pay you damages. You and your kin have already taken everything that was mine. You can't rob me twice, even if you could prove I was lying, which you can't, because every word I say is the truth."

Henry tensed, afraid Benjamin might lunge at him, even mounted as he was.

But Benjamin did not attempt to strike Gower. He sat quite still in the icy air. "The pity is that I cannot slander you, Gower," he replied. "Nothing I could say about you is untrue. You are proven a liar, a forger, and a would-be thief. You only failed at it because you were so clumsy, so damned bad at forgery that they could see at a glance that the deeds were rotten. You didn't even do it well!"

Gower's face flushed dull red, his eyes like black holes in his head. Now it was he who looked for a moment as if he would find it impossible to control his physical desire to lash out, even grasp at Benjamin and pull him off his horse. He moved, his arm out, then stopped.

"Is that what happened to Judah?" Benjamin asked, his voice grating between his teeth. "He called you a failed thief, and you lost your temper?"

Slowly Gower relaxed and a slow smile spread across his face. "I'm not sorry he's dead, Dreghorn. I'm glad. He was a corrupt man, an abuser of power and office, and there's not much worse than a judge who uses his position to steal from the men who come before him believing they'll receive justice. If the judge himself is rotten at the heart, what hope is there for the people? That is a high sin, Dreghorn. It stinks to heaven."

He stepped back, lifting his head. "But I did not kill him. He wronged me bitterly. He sent me to prison for a crime I did not commit, and he stole my inheritance from me, as well as eleven years of my life. I spoke against him, and I shall do so as long as I have breath, but I never raised my hand, or told any other man to. As far as I know, it was a just God who finally punished him. And if I wait my time, and plead my cause before the people, perhaps He'll give me back what's mine as well."

"Over my dead body!" Benjamin said bitterly. "I'll not accuse you of murder until I can prove it, but then I will. And I'll see you on the end of a rope."

"Not if there's any justice under heaven, you won't," Gower retorted. "I didn't kill him." And with a harsh, sneering smile still on his face he strode past them through the snow back toward the center of the village, the wind off the lakeshore tugging at the tails of his coat.

Benjamin watched him until he was out of sight, then he and Henry rode back toward the estate.

"I love this land," he said after a little while. "I'd forgotten how good it feels. I couldn't bear it to be poisoned by that man. I know Judah. The idea that he would be dishonest in anything is absurd. What can we do about it, Henry? How do we stop him saying these things?"

Henry had been dreading that question. "I don't know. I've been trying to think of a way, but after meeting Gower, every sort of reason seems doomed to failure. He has convinced himself that the deeds were genuine."

"That's ridiculous!" Benjamin said abruptly. "They were not only forgeries, they weren't even good ones. The expert swore to it, but anyone could have seen it when one looked. Gower's just so corroded with hatred he's lost his wits. Maybe prison has turned his mind." He looked at Henry. "You don't think he's a danger to Antonia, do you?"

Henry did not know how to answer honestly. He longed to be reassuring, but there had been a wild hatred in Ashton Gower which defied reason. He had no doubt that the man was guilty of forging in a stupid attempt to get the estate. It had apparently been such a poor attempt that any serious look at it must have told him it was not genuine. Even if Henry had not known Judah, there was the testimony of the expert. Perhaps Benjamin was right, and Gower had lost his mental balance in prison. Heaven knows, he would not be the first man to do that.

"Henry!" Benjamin said sharply.

"I don't know." Henry was forced to be honest. "I think we should warn Antonia. The servants must be told. The house must be locked securely at night. You

187

have dogs, they would warn of anyone who should not be around. It may all be unnecessary, but as long as Gower remains in the area, and in the frame of mind he is, I think it would be better."

Benjamin stopped, reining in his horse hard, and turning in the saddle. "Do you think he murdered Judah?"

It was a jarringly ugly thought, but it had been on the edge of his own mind, too. "I really don't know," Henry admitted. "I think he is an evil man, and possibly a little mad. But better we should take preventions we don't need, than that we should fail, and regret it afterwards when it is too late."

"How can we warn Antonia without frightening her?"

"I don't believe we can."

"But that's . . . God damn Gower!" Benjamin swore savagely. "God damn him to hell!"

PART TWO

*I*T STOPPED SNOWING IN THE EVENING, AND A HARD wind blew down the lake, whining in the eaves and rattling the windows. But in the morning when Henry pulled the curtains, even before Mrs. Hardcastle came with tea, there were bare patches on the north and west faces of the hills, and lower down the snow had drifted deep against walls and fences.

The postmaster arrived after breakfast with a telegraph message from Ephraim, sent the day before from Lancaster, to say that he would be arriving on the midday train. The lawyer also rode up from the village, before going on to Penrith, to speak about the estate to Antonia and Benjamin. Therefore, it was again Henry who stood on the platform when the train came in, belching steam into the air, and nearly an hour late because of snow drifting over Shap Fell.

He saw Ephraim immediately. He was as tall as Benjamin, but leaner. And he walked with a loose, easy gait in spite of the cold. He carried only one case; it was quite large, but in his hand it seemed to have no weight at all. Like Benjamin he was burned by the sun and wind, and frowned very slightly as he saw no one he was expecting on the platform waiting for him. He glanced up at the sky, perhaps fearing the snow had been worse here, and he would not be able to go farther until it cleared.

"Ephraim!" Henry called out. "Ephraim!"

Ephraim turned, startled at first, then his face lit when he recognized Henry, and he dropped the case and came forward to clasp Henry's hand.

"Rathbone! How are you? What are you doing here? You've come to stay with us over Christmas? That's wonderful. It's going to be like old times. You look cold, and sort of pinched. Where is everyone? Where's Judah? Have you been waiting long?"

"Not on the platform," Henry answered with a smile. "I've been at the inn with a pint of Cockerhoop." That was the light ale that was so popular locally. He felt a lift of gratitude that Ephraim could welcome him so generously at what had been intended as a family reunion. He was, after all, not a Dreghorn, merely Antonia's godfather, an honorary position, not one of kinship. He dreaded having to tell him the real reason he was here; his stomach knotted up and his throat was tight. Was it better to crush his pleasure immediately with honesty, or allow a little time, let him take joy in homecoming first?

Ephraim was smiling broadly. He was quieter than his brother, a man of deep thoughts he shared seldom, and great physical courage. Whatever fears or doubts he had about anything, he mastered them without outer show. But after being in Africa for four years, the sight of his beloved lakes again woke a joy in him that found expression easily.

"Sounds perfect," he said with enthusiasm. "We'll go for some long walks in the snow, climb a bit even, and then sit by a roaring fire and talk about dreams and tell each other tall stories. I've got a few. Henry, there are things in Africa you wouldn't believe!" He picked up his case and matched Henry stride for stride out to the waiting trap which Wiggins had brought around ready when he heard the train draw in.

"How's Judah?" Ephraim asked as soon as they were in the trap and moving. "Have you heard from Ben yet? And Naomi? Is she coming, too?" There was an eagerness in his voice when he mentioned her name, and he turned away as if to guard the emotion in his eyes from being seen.

Thoughts teemed through Henry's mind, an awareness that there was a new dimension he had not even thought of, and pain he would not be able to read in Ephraim as well as he had in Benjamin, depths he could neither understand nor help. And yet there was no alternative. Now was the moment.

"Benjamin is already here," he answered the easiest question first. "He arrived two days ago . . ."

Ephraim turned toward him, blue eyes puzzled. "Is he all right?"

"No," Henry said frankly. "We are none of us all right. Judah died in an accident eight days ago." He looked at Ephraim's face as the shock struck him, followed by disbelief, then pain. "I am sorry I am the one to tell you, but the lawyer called this morning regarding certain estate matters, and Benjamin stayed with Antonia to see him."

"Hunting?" Ephraim said hoarsely. Judah seldom hunted, but it was the only way to keep foxes down in the Lakeland, and they devastated sheep if left. Ewes and lambs had their throats torn out, whole flocks of chickens could be slaughtered.

"No," Henry replied, and told him briefly all they knew so far.

Ephraim huddled into his coat as if suddenly the wind cut through it and it was no protection to his body. "Where on earth was he going?" he asked huskily. "At night?"

"We don't know. He said it was just to get a little air before going to bed. They had all been at the village listening to a visiting musician. A violinist. He had actually played a small piece Joshua had written."

"Joshua?" Ephraim repeated the name. "Judah said he was brilliant. He was so proud of him." He controlled himself with difficulty. There was nothing in his face, but his voice broke. "I brought something for Joshua from Africa. Seems irrelevant now."

"It won't be, later," Henry assured him. "Benjamin brought him a beautiful gift also, a piece of scripture, original, in a carved wooden box."

"I brought him a chief's necklace of office, an African version of a crown," Ephraim said. "It's made of gold and ivory. At a glance it seems barbaric, but when you look more closely it's very beautifully carved. Nothing like European at all. I suppose you are right, and in time he will like it. Today it'll seem utterly pointless."

"That is not all I need to tell you before we get to the house," Henry went on. They were making quite good speed. The wind had cleared most of the snow off the road. There were one or two places where it had drifted, and they got out and took the spades from the space where the luggage was and helped Wiggins dig a path. Henry saw Ephraim attack the heavy piles with an energy born of anger, his back bent, his weight thrown behind each shovelful. Then they put the spades back and climbed up again to go forward. It was necessary only three times.

"What else?" Ephraim asked without interest when they were on their way again and the broad, white-flecked surface of the lake lay ahead.

"Ashton Gower is out of prison and saying that he was wrongly convicted. The deeds were genuine, and Judah knew it," Henry answered, pulling the rug a little tighter around both of them. His feet were wet, as were the bottoms of his trousers.

"That's nonsense." Ephraim dismissed it as of no worth, even to discuss.

"I know it is nonsense," Henry agreed. "But he is repeating it very insistently, and Benjamin feels it is important that he is stopped. There are many people in the village who were not there at the time of the trial, and don't know the truth. He is being offensive, and causing Antonia some distress. We cannot ignore him." He did not add that Benjamin suspected the possibility of his having been involved in Judah's death. Ephraim was not as easy for him to read, and he was uncertain of his anger, or the depth of his pain.

Ephraim did not reply for some time, at least another hundred yards farther along the road. Now the white roofs of the village houses were clear in the hard light and the trees were dense black against the gray water.

"Henry, are you saying that there are people who believe him?" he asked at length. "How could anyone who knew Judah at all consider such a thing even for a moment? There was never a more honest man than he, and Ashton Gower is a vicious cur, without honor, kindness, or any other redeeming virtue. Who is there anywhere that can say he has done them a good turn without expecting payment for it?"

"I know it, Ephraim," Henry replied. "I think per- haps prison turned his mind. But it doesn't change the fact that he is furious, and bent on clearing his name, whatever the cost."

"You speak as if you believe he is a danger," Ephraim said gravely. "Is he?"

Henry was compelled to admit it. "I don't know. Benjamin thinks it is possible he had a hand in Judah's death. I cannot discount it, either. We met him in the village yesterday, and he has a hatred in him that chilled me. We have told the household servants to be careful locking everything, and to leave the dogs loose at night. It is deeply unpleasant, Ephraim. We can't leave the Lakes, and Antonia and Joshua alone, with this unexplained." He looked at Ephraim's face, pale under the African sunburn. "I'm sorry. I wish I could have told you better things."

Ephraim put his hand on Henry's arm and clasped it hard. "The truth, Henry. That is all that will serve us. Thank you for coming. We shall need your help."

Henry did not say that they had it; Ephraim knew that.

It was a quiet, somber evening, rain and snow alternately beating against the windows and the fire roaring in the hearth. They ate Lakeland mutton and sweet, earth-flavored potatoes with herbs mixed in.

Spices were imported along the coast, and Cumberland gingerbread was famous. Hot, with cream, it made an excellent pudding.

Ephraim and Benjamin spoke quietly together, sharing memories, and Henry sat by the fire with Antonia, mostly listening to whatever she wanted to say, and when she preferred, telling her tales of London and the busy city life that she had never experienced.

*H*enry slept well, tired after the drive through the wind and snow to Penrith, but he woke early, while it was still dark. He did not wish to lie in bed any longer, and he rose and dressed warmly and was outside before the dawn.

By the time the sun rose over the mountains to the southwest, and spread soft, pearly light through a mackerel sky, he was more than halfway to the stepping-stones at the upper crossing where Judah had died.

Thoughts whirled in his mind as he trudged over the crisp unbroken snow, splashed pink by the sun. Was he imagining the emotion in Ephraim's voice as he asked if Nathaniel's widow was coming as well? Even as he asked himself the question, the certainty of the answer was in his mind: Ephraim himself had been in love with her then, and the memory of it was sharp still.

Of course he would not have seen her since the last time they had both been home, which, as far as Henry knew, was seven years ago. People could change a great deal in such a time. Experience could refine their feelings, or obliterate them.

Henry had not met her, and knew nothing except that she was English, from the east coast, and Nathaniel had known her for only a few months before marrying her. They had left for America shortly after that. Antonia had spoken warmly of her; Judah had seemed to have some reservations, but he had not said what they were. Had they been only an awareness that his youngest brother had loved her as well?

He was making his way downhill very slightly now, being careful not to slip. The stream lay ahead of him, running fast. The recent snow had added to it; it washed almost to the top of the stepping-stones placed across it, ten in all, flat, carefully chosen.

Where the stream had carved little bays and hollows out of the bank the current had carried ice down and left it, glittering in the broadening light. The far bank rose more steeply. Henry looked from left to right, but there was nothing except faint indentations where sheep had made tracks for themselves. What on earth would bring Judah here, at night? To be alone with thoughts that troubled him so intensely he could not address them in the house, with Antonia present? Or to meet someone?

Had he been afraid of Ashton Gower and the damage he could cause? Had Gower threatened Antonia, or even Joshua? Would Judah have considered paying him in some way, to protect them?

That was nothing like the man Henry had known. But do people change when those they love are threatened?

He stared up and down the swollen stream. In the daylight he could see the fall clearly, the water splashing white over the jagged rocks. They were certainly sharp enough to have caused the injuries Leighton had described. Everything fitted with the facts. Ice on the stones, one false step, poor balance, even simple tiredness, and a fall could cause a blow that would render one senseless. Facedown and one could drown in minutes—the water did not need to be deep. The current could carry a body down to the fall and cause the lacerations Leighton spoke of.

But knowing Gower, why on earth would Judah meet him here, alone at night? The answer was simple. He would not. And to suppose chance, made no sense either. Gower would not wait here on a bitter, winter night in case Judah came! That was absurd.

Ashton Gower might well have wished him dead, and rejoiced when he was, but there was nothing whatever to suggest that he had killed him, except the madness of the man and his hunger for revenge, and they proved nothing at all.

Reluctantly he turned and made his way back, shivering in spite of his coat, scarf, hat, and thick, fur-lined gloves. Everything in him wanted to believe Gower was responsible. It was factually absurd, and emotionally the only thing that made sense.

With the daylight the snow was thawing and by the time he reached the house his feet were thoroughly soaked, as were the bottoms of his trousers. He went up the back stairs to his room and changed before coming down again to the dining room.

Mrs. Hardcastle brought him a late breakfast, and he was joined by Benjamin, curious to know where he had been.

"To the stepping-stones," Henry replied when asked. "Tea?"

Benjamin sat down. He looked tired, his eyes hollowed round with shadows. He accepted the offer. Henry poured for them. "Why?"

"Just to see if what Leighton told us makes sense. It does, Ben. I can't imagine Judah going there to meet Gower at night, and it's ridiculous to think Gower waited there for him by chance."

Benjamin looked at him steadily. "You think it was simply an accident?"

Henry did not know how to answer. His intelligence and his instinct fought against each other. He was a man used to logical thought, brought up in the discipline and the beauty of reason. And yet his knowledge of Judah Dreghorn made the deductions sit ill with him. He answered the only way honesty could dictate. "There must be something we don't know, perhaps several things."

Benjamin gave a rueful smile. "Same old Henry, careful thinker." He drew in a deep breath and let it out in a sigh. "We need that now more than ever. What do we tell Antonia?"

Henry did not have to weigh his answer. There was only one they could afford, and he had a firmer trust of Antonia's courage and judgment than Benjamin had, sharp memories of her frankness, her curiosity, and the courage with which she met the answers, so many of which she had had to face alone. It hurt him deeply that her happiness had been so short. "The truth," he replied.

The opportunity did not come until the evening. Either one of them had been otherwise occupied, or Joshua had been with them, but after dinner they were all gathered around the fire, and Joshua had gone to bed. It was Benjamin who began, looking at Antonia with grave apology.

"I'm sorry to raise it again, but I believe we need to understand better what happened the night Judah died."

"I don't know anything I haven't told you," she answered, her hands knotted in her lap, unornamented but for her gold wedding ring.

He was gentle. "What did you talk about on the way home from the recital?"

"The music, of course."

"How was Judah? Of course he would be proud of Joshua, but was he otherwise just as usual?"

She considered for a few moments. "Looking back on it, he was more than usually absorbed in thought. I believed at the time it was the emotion of the music, and that perhaps he was tired. He had had a difficult case in Penrith. I didn't know then just how awful Gower had been. Judah had not told me, I only learned after his death of the details. He's an evil man, Benjamin. To hate so much is a kind of insanity, I think, and that is frightening."

"Did Judah mention him at all? Can you remember?"

Ephraim sat motionless, his face deep in thought. Henry felt a chill of anxiety. There was a power in Ephraim, a courage that stopped at nothing. If he once were convinced that Ashton Gower had killed his brother, nothing would deter him from pursuing justice. Such strength was disturbing.

"When I think of it," Antonia replied, "he actually spoke very little. He only answered me."

"He didn't say where he was going, or why he wanted to walk at that hour?" Benjamin persisted.

"Not really, just for the air," she answered. She looked uncertain. "I thought he wanted to think."

"Outside, on a winter night?"

She said nothing, now deeply unhappy.

Henry was gentler. "Did he suggest you should not wait up for him?"

She had to think for a moment. "Yes. Yes, he did say something like that. I don't remember exactly what."

"So he expected to be gone an hour or more," Henry deduced.

"An hour?" Benjamin questioned.

"By the time Joshua had got over his excitement and gone to bed, and then Antonia herself had," Henry replied. "It sounds as if he intended to go as far as the stream. What lies beyond it? Where is this Viking site, exactly?"

"Farther down the stream," she said. "Just above the lower crossing before you get to the church. He wasn't going to the site. There's nothing really beyond the higher crossing, except a copse of trees, and a shepherd's hut. Do you suppose he was going there? What for?"

There was only one answer, and it hung in the air like an additional darkness.

"If it was someone he didn't trust, he'd have taken the dogs. They'd have attacked anyone who threatened him."

"Or he was going to see someone he trusted," Henry said.

Antonia stared at the fire. "Or there was no one else. He slipped, that's all, just as Dr. Leighton said."

Benjamin's face was bleak. "Which could not have been Gower. We are no further forward."

Another thought occurred to Henry. "Unless he went with the purpose of helping Gower, perhaps to offer him some kind of assistance in getting himself work, or some establishment in the community again."

Ephraim's eyes opened wide. "After what Gower had been saying about him? But if he was, why there, of all places? And in the middle of the night!"

"Judah might have helped him anyway," Antonia said quietly. "He helped all kinds of people. But I can't think why meet there!"

"Neither can I," Benjamin agreed coldly. "What happened? Gower killed him for his trouble? Or else when Judah slipped, just left him there to drown? I know the man was a swine, but that's inhuman."

"If he did, we'll prove it." Ephraim stared at him. "I'll see him answer for every word, every act. He'll never blacken a Dreghorn name again."

Antonia smiled and nodded, her eyes brimming with tears.

But alone upstairs in his room, Henry looked out of the window toward the vast, snow-bleached expanse of the mountains under the star-glittered sky, and thought what he had not dared say to the family. He had known Judah well, they had been friends for years, shared all manner of things both with words and in silence. They had understood the emotions that were too complicated to explain, and talked all night of the philosophies that lent themselves to end-less exploration.

Judah would not have met alone with Ashton Gower to offer him help, after Gower had accused him of fraud, at the stream or anywhere else. He was far too sophisticated not to realize that Gower could then blackmail him with the threat that he had helped only to hide his own guilt, and Gower would do that. That was the kind of man he was, and Judah knew it.

The more Henry weighed the facts they had, the less any answer fitted them. Each one left loose ends and questions unanswered. He drew the curtains across and prepared to go to bed. Tomorrow he would have one more journey to make to the station at Penrith, and one more time to break the news.

*I*n the morning the thaw had set in and everything was dripping. Much of the snow had melted and there were long streaks of black over the hills where the slopes were bare. Trees that had been hung with icicles yesterday were naked today, branches an unen-cumbered lace against the sky.

A grim-faced Mrs. Hardcastle served breakfast of eggs, bacon, Cumberland sausage, toast, jam made of witherslacks, or brambles known as black kite, and scalding hot tea in a silver pot. The reason for her anger became known quite early on: Ashton Gower had resumed his accusation and one of the newcomers in the village was repeating it. Mrs. Hardcastle's opinion of her should have turned the milk sour.

Henry was ready to set out for the station when Ephraim strode across the stable yard, coattails flapping, and climbed in beside him. He offered no explanation and Henry made no remark. He had a strong idea why Ephraim had come, and he was not sure whether it would make the task of breaking the news to Naomi Dreghorn easier or more difficult. He half expected Ephraim to offer to go in his place, but he did not. It seemed that in this first meeting again after the years between, and Nathaniel's death, he did not wish to be alone with Naomi.

There was little wind, but the damp in the air made the journey cold. Neither of them had anything further to say about Gower or the subject of his accusations. Henry asked Ephraim about Africa, and was caught up out of the grief of the moment listening to his answers.

Ephraim smiled, and for a space of time he did not see the sweep of snow-scattered hills or the ragged clouds above, but felt the hot sun on his skin and dry winds of Africa carrying the scents of dust and animal dung, eyes narrowed against the light as he saw in his mind's eye the endless plains with vast herds of beasts and the curious flat-topped acacia trees.

"You can hear the lions roar in the night," he said with a smile. "It's primeval nature as you never see it in Europe. We've grown old and become too civilized. You hear a hyena's maniacal laughter in the dark, and it's as if you heard the first joke at the beginning of the world, and he's the only one who knows it."

For a moment Henry also forgot the knife-edge wind with the rain behind it.

"And the plants," Ephraim went on. "Every shape and color imaginable, and nothing lost or wasted, nothing without a use. It is so superb that sometimes I feel drunk just looking at it."

They continued to talk.

The time of the journey flew by, and because of the change in the weather, the train pulled in within moments of midday. There were clouds of steam, shouts, and a clanging of doors.

Henry did not know Naomi by sight. He realized with surprise that he did not even know what manner of woman to expect. He had been too preoccupied with present events even to form a picture in his mind, tall or short, dark or fair. Now he stood on the platform without any idea at all.

Five women alighted from the train. Two were elderly, and accompanied by men, a third was dark and spare with a grim countenance and severe clothes as if she were applying for a place as a governess in some forbidding establishment. Henry knew Ephraim well enough to not even consider her.

The other two were handsome, the first fair-haired and dainty, a most feminine woman. She looked about her as if searching for a familiar face.

Henry was about to go forward, certain this must be Naomi; then he saw the other young woman. She was taller, broader of shoulder, and she walked with an extraordinary grace, as if movement were a pleasure to her, an unconsidered and natural art. Her face had an unusual beauty, partly a strength of feature, but even more an intelligence, as if everything were of interest to her. If she had ever felt fear, there was no mark of it in her bearing. Henry could not help wondering if it was complete innocence, or a most remarkable courage.

He looked sideways, momentarily at Ephraim, and the last doubt vanished that this was Naomi.

Henry stepped forward. "Naomi Dreghorn?"

She smiled at him, charming but cool. She did not know him, and for a moment it seemed that she had not recognized Ephraim either.

"My name is Henry Rathbone," he introduced himself. "I have come to meet you and take you to the house. You may remember, it is about six miles away, on the lake."

"How do you do, Mr. Rathbone." Her smile was wide and full of pleasure, and she offered him her hand, as if she had been a man. It was slim and strong, and she gripped his firmly.

He picked up her case. "And I expect you remember Ephraim?"

Her face was calm, but the warmth in it was suddenly distant.

"Of course. How are you, Ephraim?"

He replied a little stiffly. She might have thought it was coolness, but Henry could see the uncharacteristic awkwardness of his movement—his usual ease which had its own kind of grace was entirely vanished. He was at a disadvantage which was unfamiliar to him.

They spoke of trivialities until they were seated in the trap and on their way out of Penrith and once again going westward, the damp wind in their faces, smelling of rain.

Ephraim asked Naomi about America, sounding as if it were mere courtesy that made him inquire. She replied warmly, with imagination and wit, so that whether he would or not, he was compelled to care. She described the vast plains of the west, the herds of buffalo that made the earth tremble when they ran, the high deserts to which she had traveled from the west, where the earth was red and ochre and the colors of fire, wind-eroded to fantastic shapes, like castles and towers of the imagination.

She did not speak of Nathaniel's death, and neither Henry nor Ephraim asked, each waiting for the other to broach the subject of death, and break the news to her. They had half an hour's truce with death while she described travel and adventure, hardship made the best of, and they found themselves laughing.

"I brought a gift for Joshua," she said with a smile that held a trace of self-mockery. "I think I chose it because I like it myself rather than because he will, but I didn't mean it to be so. I like to give people things I would keep."

"What is it?" Henry asked with genuine interest. What would this most unusual woman have brought, to go with Benjamin's scripture in its carved and perfumed case, and Ephraim's royal necklace of ivory and gold?

"An hourglass," she replied. "A memento mori, I suppose you would call it. A reminder of death—and the infinite value of life. It is made of crystal and set with semiprecious stones of the desert. The sand that runs through it is red, from the valleys that look like fire."

"It sounds perfect." Henry meant it. "We spend too much of our lives dreaming of the past or the future. There is a sense in which the present is all we have, and we cannot hold it dearly enough. It sounds like a gift of both beauty and memory, like the other gifts he has been brought."

"You think so?" She seemed to care for his opinion.

If Ephraim was not going to tell her, then he must.

"I do. But before we reach the village, I am afraid there is hard news we have to share."

"What is it?" She saw that it was serious and the light vanished from her face.

Briefly he told her about Judah's death and Ashton Gower's accusations.

She listened very gravely, and spoke only when he had finished, by which time they were less than a mile from the house.

"What are we going to do about it?" she asked, looking first at Henry, then at Ephraim. "This man must be silenced from slander, and if he is in any way responsible for Judah's death, then we must see that he answers for it! Apart from justice, Antonia and Joshua are not safe unless he is imprisoned again, and his words shown as lies."

This time it was Ephraim who answered. "We have to prove he was there," he said grimly. "It isn't going to be easy because he will have made sure he told no one, and no one else would be out at such a place at night."

"Why else would Judah go out there in the snow at night, except to meet somebody?" she asked.

There was no answer, and they were approaching the drive gates.

The next hour was taken up in the emotion of arrival and welcome, exchanges of concern, of grief, and of a depth of understanding between the two women, who had both experienced widowhood while still so young. Although they had known each other only briefly, and that several years ago, there was an ease in their communication as if friendship were natural.

They resumed the conversation in the late afternoon over tea by the fire with scones, hinberry jam, and slices of ginger cake, baked with spices and rich molasses from the West Indies.

This time Antonia joined in. "The more I think of it, the more certain I am that he intended to meet someone," she said gravely. "I hadn't remembered before, but he took out his pocket watch several times in order to check the time. I thought then that it was to see how long the recital had been, but he would not do that more than once."

"The difficulty will be to prove that it was Gower," Benjamin pointed out. "It is not the easiest place for them to meet, and frankly, a ridiculous time."

"But Judah was there!" Antonia argued. "However absurd it is, it is the truth."

"There is still something we do not know," Henry insisted. "Either something important, or that we have misunderstood, and it is not what it seems."

Ephraim's face set hard. "Well, two things I am sure of: Judah would not have done anything unjust or dishonest; and the other is that Ashton Gower is a convicted forger, driven by hate and the passion for revenge on the family who legitimately bought his estate. Judah is dead, and Gower is alive and slandering his name."

"None of that is at issue," Benjamin agreed. "The problem is to prove it." He turned to Antonia. "What was Judah wearing that night?"

She looked puzzled. "It was an evening recital. We were all dressed quite formally."

"He didn't change before he went out afterwards?"

"No." She bit her lip. "I assumed he simply wanted to walk a little after sitting in the hall all evening, and in the carriage on the way back. Why? How can that help?"

"I don't know," Benjamin admitted. "But there is no point in trying to find anything on the ground where it happened. All marks or prints will have disappeared long ago. His clothes will have been kept safely. I thought there might be something, a tear, even a note of a meeting, anything at all . . ." He tailed off, losing belief in the hope as he spoke.

"There could be a note," Henry said, rising to his feet. "Sometimes things remain dry inside a pocket. If anything at all is legible, it might help. Let us at least look."

"Of course," Antonia agreed, standing also. "I didn't know what else to do with them. I couldn't bring myself even to clean them . . ." She gave a brief, tight little smile. "Maybe it is for the best?"

They followed her up the stairs and across the landing to Judah's dressing room. Henry found it disturbing to go into a dead man's private space, see his hairbrushes and collar studs set out on the tallboy, cuff links in boxes, shoes and boots on their racks. His razor was set beside an empty bowl and ewer in front of the looking glass in which he must have seen his face so many times.

He glanced quickly at Benjamin, and saw reflected in his expression exactly the emotions he felt himself, the grief, the slight embarrassment as if they had intruded when Judah was no longer capable of stopping them. It was uncomfortable for reasons he had not expected.

In Antonia he saw only the pain of her loneliness. She must have been in here many times before.

Ephraim, several years younger than Judah, carried his loss inside him, concealed as much as he was able. His face was tight, muscles pulling his mouth into a thinner line, eyes avoiding others.

Naomi put her arm around Antonia. She had perhaps done exactly this same grim task, and knew how it felt.

It was left to Henry to go to the top of the chest of drawers where the dark suit was folded, dry and stiff from river water and heavy traces of sand and silt. He opened the jacket and looked at it carefully. It had been little worn, perhaps no more than a year or two old, and made of excellent quality wool. It was beautiful cloth, probably from the fleeces of Lakeland sheep, but the label inside was that of a Liverpool tailor. It told him nothing at all, except the taste of the man who had worn it, which he already knew.

Then he looked in the pockets one by one. He found a handkerchief, stained by water, but still folded, so probably otherwise clean. There were two business cards, a shirt maker in Penrith and a saddler in Kendal. In the wallet there were papers, some of which looked like receipts, but were too smudged to read, a treasury note for five pounds—a lot of money; not that anyone had assumed robbery. The last item was a penknife with a mother-of-pearl handle set with a silver, initialed shield. Presumably any coins would be in his trouser pockets. Henry was about to look when Antonia's voice stopped him.

"What's that?" she said sharply. "The knife?"

He held it up. "This? A penknife. He would have one, to sharpen a quill." It was a very usual thing to carry. He did not understand the strain and disbelief in her face.

"That one!" she exclaimed, holding out her hand.

He passed it to her.

She turned it over, her eyes wide, her skin bleached of color.

"What is it, Antonia?" Benjamin asked. "Why does it matter? Isn't it Judah's?"

"Yes." She looked at each of them in turn. "He lost it the day before he died." The words seemed to catch in her throat.

Benjamin frowned. "Well, he must have found it

again. It's easy enough to misplace something so small."

"Where did he lose it?" Henry asked her.

"That's what I mean." She stared at him. "In the stream. He was bending over and it fell out of his pocket. He searched for it, we both did, but we couldn't find it again."

Ephraim said what Henry was thinking. "Maybe that's why he went back the night he died." It was obvious in his face and his voice that he loathed admitting it, but honesty compelled him. "It's a very nice knife. And it has his initials on it. Perhaps it was a gift, and he cared very much about losing it."

"I gave it to him," Antonia said. "But he didn't lose it at the stones where he was found." She had to stop a moment to struggle for control of her voice.

There was utter silence in the small dressing room. No one moved. No one asked.

"It was by the bridge a mile and a half farther down. The two stones set across the water above it."

"Farther down!" Benjamin was incredulous. "That doesn't make any sense. It . . ." He did not say it.

Henry knew what they were all thinking. It was in their faces as it was in his mind. Bodies do not wash upstream, only down.

"Are you absolutely certain?" he said quietly.

"Yes."

It was the proof they needed. Judah had been

moved after he was dead, and left where it looked as if he had fallen accidentally.

"Are there any sharp rocks at the lower bridge where he lost the knife?" Henry pressed.

"No! Just water, deep . . . and gravel." Antonia closed her eyes. "He was murdered . . . wasn't he?"

Henry looked at Benjamin, then at Ephraim, then at last back at Antonia.

"Yes. I can think of no other explanation." He felt stunned by the reality of it. Judah's death had made no sense and they had all been convinced that Ashton Gower was capable of murder. Henry had believed it himself. But it was still different now that it was no longer theoretical but something from which there was no escape.

"What are we going to do?" Naomi asked. "How do we prove that it was Gower? Where do we begin?"

Ephraim put his hand up and pushed his hair back slowly off his brow. His eyes were unfocused, staring at something within himself.

Benjamin looked at Antonia, then at Henry. There was horror in his eyes and a deep, painful confusion. Death had hurt him, as he had expected it would, as Nathaniel's death had, but hatred and murder were apart from all he had known. They looked to Henry because he was older. He had an inner calm that concealed his emotions, and he did not betray the pain or the ignorance inside him. He had come to terms with it long ago.

"Tomorrow, when it's light," he replied. "We should go to the place where Judah lost the knife, and therefore found it, and see if we can learn anything. We can at least see how long it would take anyone to carry a body from there, upstream to the place he was found, and then go back to the village. If we follow in the steps of whoever did it, we may learn something about them."

"Yes," Benjamin agreed. "That's where we should begin. In the morning."

*T*hey set out together after breakfast. The light was glittering sharp, the lake gray, with silver shadows like strokes from a giant brush. Underfoot the ice crackled with every step, hung in bright strands from the branches of every tree. The wind drifted ragged clouds, tearing them high, like mares' tails.

They set out walking, Henry and Benjamin ahead, Ephraim alone after them, Antonia and Naomi last, high leather boots keeping their feet dry. No amount of care could keep their skirts from being sodden by the loose snow.

The route to the lower crossing was actually easier. They stood on the bank and stared at the wild, almost colorless landscape. Everything was black rocks, shining water, and bleached snow. Of course it would be possible to fall off the stones, but if one did, it would be far from any jagged edges. There were no rocks, no race or fall to cause the injuries Judah had suffered. The bottom of the stream here was pebbles and larger, smooth stones.

"That proves it," Ephraim said grimly. "He couldn't have fallen accidentally and hit his head here. Someone killed him, and then carried or dragged him upstream to where he was found." He looked along the bank as he said it, and everyone else's eyes followed his.

"How?" Benjamin asked the obvious question. The ground rose sharply, and a hundred yards away there was a copse of trees straddling both sides. There was no path, not even a sheep track. "How could anyone carry a grown man's body along there, let alone a big man like Judah?"

"On a horse," Naomi said quickly. "That's the only possible way. It's steep, rough, and uphill." She looked at Antonia. "A horse would leave marks in the snow, at both places. We can't find out now about this place, but Wiggins would remember if there were prints of a horse's hooves where Judah was found."

"There was nothing," Ephraim answered for her. "I asked, because I wanted to prove that he went there to meet someone."

"Did it snow any more on that night to fill them in?" Benjamin asked.

"No." This time it was Antonia who spoke. "If there were no prints, then there can't have been anyone else there. You can't walk on snow without leaving a mark, whoever you are." There was pain in her voice, as if a vestige of sense had been snatched from her just when she had thought she understood.

"But he was killed here!" Ephraim insisted. "Nothing floats upstream!"

"Water," Henry said aloud.

Ephraim's face tightened, his eyes as cold and blue as the sky. "Water does not flow upstream, Henry," he said bitterly. He only just refrained from adding that the remark was stupid and unhelpful, but it was in his expression.

"You can walk in water without leaving a mark," Henry corrected him. He turned to look up the slope again. "You could drag a body up the river, walking on the bed and letting the water itself help bear the weight. It's only a mile or so. You'd leave no trace, and it's extremely unlikely anyone would see you. Even if anyone were out, the bed is low-lying naturally, because the stream has cut it. Anything you disturbed would look as if the current did it, and if anyone did come in the light of the half moon, you would see them black against the snow. And if you bent over, you would simply look like an outcrop of rock, an edge of the bank."

221

Benjamin breathed out gently. "Why didn't I think of that? It's a superb answer. The clever swine! How can we prove it?"

"We can't." Ephraim bit his lip. "That's why it's so extremely clever. Sorry, Henry."

Henry brushed the apology aside with a smile. "What I don't understand is how Judah lost the penknife the first time, and couldn't find it, yet the second time, in the dark and when he must have had other things on his mind, he saw it!" He looked around at the snow-covered bark, the water clear as glass above the stones, and the dark, roughly cut edges of the stones used for the bridge. They were carefully wedged so they would not slip, even with a man's weight on them.

"Where did he drop it?" Benjamin asked Antonia.

"He bent forward to look at his boot," she replied. "He thought he might have cut the leather, but it was only scuffed."

"And where did you look?"

"On the path, in the snow, and at the edge of the water, in case it went in. The mother-of-pearl would have caught the light," she replied.

Henry looked at the bridge stones where they were wedged. "Did he put his foot up here to look at the boot?"

"Yes. Oh!" Antonia's face lit. "You mean it fell between the stones there? And perhaps he remembered . . ."

"Is it possible?" He knew from her face that it was.

Ephraim turned his face toward the stream. "Do you suppose Gower took the horse up there, with Judah slung across it?"

They all followed his eyes, seeing the winding course of it, the deeps and shallows.

"Possibly," Henry answered. "Or left it here, and walked, dragging him. Neither would be easy, and it would have taken far longer than we originally thought. He must have been away from home a good deal of the night, and half dead with cold after going a mile or more upstream, up to his thighs in icy water, either leading the horse, which would have been reluctant, or dragging the body. And then he had to tramp home through the snow. I wouldn't be surprised if his feet were frostbitten by it."

"Good!" Ephraim snapped. "I hope he loses his toes."

"He wouldn't risk going to Leighton with it," Benjamin said thoughtfully. The wind was rising and over to the west the sky was gray. "There's more snow coming," he went on. "We know now what happened. We can make plans what to do best at home. Come on." And he turned and started to lead the way back again, offering his arm to Antonia.

*A*fter having taken off their wet clothes, they assembled around the fire. Mrs. Hardcastle brought them hot cocoa and ginger cake, then they set about the serious discussion of what they could each do to bring Ashton Gower to justice.

No one questioned that Benjamin had a high intelligence, a keen and orderly mind that, if he governed the overriding emotion of outrage, he could use to direct the investigation. He could make sense of all they could learn and integrate it into one story to lay before the authorities. His leadership was taken for granted.

Ephraim had courage and a power that would accept no defeat as sufficient to deflect him from his purpose. Now they were certain that there was a crime to solve, his strength would be invaluable.

It was Henry who suggested that they should also make use of Naomi's charm to gain what might otherwise be beyond their reach. Laughter and a quick smile often achieved what demand could not, and she agreed immediately, as keen as anyone else to help.

Antonia, newly widowed and with such a young child, was required by custom and decorum to remain at home. Apart from that, she had no desire at all to leave Joshua with a governess or tutor while he puzzled as to what all the adults were doing, knowing something was desperately wrong, but not told what it was, or how they hoped to resolve it. However, her reputation and the regard she had earned in her years in the village would stand well in their favor.

"We will take luncheon early and begin this afternoon," Benjamin declared. His face was grave as he turned to Ephraim. "There is at least one man in the village who knows what manner of man Gower is, and that is Colgrave. He is not an easy man to like, but he is our best ally in this. Go to him and gain as much of his help as you can. He won't find it hard to believe that Gower could have killed Judah, but don't raise that question unless he does. Remember that we have two objectives: to establish exactly how Judah died." His mouth pinched tight and his eyes were full of anger. He was finding it hard to control the pain of loss he felt. Judah had been his beloved and admired elder brother. His memories were full of laughter, adventure, and friendship. To have a creature like Ashton Gower not only end the future but sully the past as well was almost insupportable. "And to prove it and find justice for him," he went on. "But we must also silence his lies forever and show to everyone that all he says is false. Colgrave might be able to help in both. But be careful how you ask."

Ephraim's mouth turned down at the corners. "Don't worry, I shan't trust him," he replied. "But he'll help me with everything he can, I promise you."

Benjamin turned to Naomi. "Henry and I already spoke to Gower. We met him by chance in the street. He's consumed with hatred. Even death isn't enough to satisfy him. He wants to justify himself and get the estate back for . . ."

"I'll see him in hell first," Ephraim said huskily.

"There's no good confronting him," Benjamin argued. "We need to determine where he was that night, and if it was even possible for him to have been to the crossing where Judah was killed, and also the stones where he was found. Does he have access to a horse, or did he take one? Did anyone see him, and if so, where and at what time? If we gain anything from him it will be either by charm, or tricking him. Naomi . . ."

"No!" Ephraim cut across him, instantly protective. "You can't ask her to speak to him. For God's sake, Ben, he murdered Judah!"

Naomi flushed, seeing the emotion in Ephraim's face.

"He won't know who she is," Benjamin pointed out, apparently oblivious of it, or of her embarrassment. He could think only of plans. "And if she went with Henry . . ."

"I'd rather go alone," Naomi said quickly. She flashed a smile at Henry, as if he would understand, then looked back at Benjamin. "To begin with at least, I can pretend anything I wish, or allow him to assume it. If I go with Mr. Rathbone, Gower will take against me from the outset, because he knows Mr. Rathbone is your friend."

"He's dangerous," Ephraim told her, finality in his

voice. "You forget where he's been already. He was eleven years in prison in Carlisle. He's not a . . ."

She looked at him with the shadow of a smile on her mouth, but her eyes were direct, even challenging. Watching them, Henry realized that there was far more between them than he, or Benjamin, had supposed, and a great deal more emotion.

"We suspect that he murdered a member of our family," she replied coolly. "I understand that, Ephraim. I am going to see him openly, and in daylight. He is evil, we are all perfectly certain of that, but he is not stupid. If he were, we would not find him so difficult to catch."

The dull red of anger spread up Ephraim's cheeks, and a consciousness that he was betraying his emotion too far. It was as if their exchange was not new but merely something in the middle of an established difference.

Benjamin looked at his brother, then at his sister-in-law, aware that he had missed something, but not certain what it was. "Are you sure you would not prefer to have Henry with you?" he asked.

"Quite sure," Naomi answered. "If Gower sees me with anyone from this house we will in a sense have tipped our hands." She looked at Antonia, and bit her lip. "Sorry. That is a card-playing expression I have heard men use. I'm afraid I have mixed with some odd company when traveling. Geological sites are not always in the most civilized of places."

Antonia smiled for the first time since Henry had arrived, perhaps since Judah's death. "Please don't apologize. Some time, when this is past, I would like to hear more about it. There are advantages to having a family, but there are chances you lose as well. But I understand the reference. You might be surprised how fierce and how devious some of the ladies of the village can be about their cards."

Now it was Naomi who smiled self-consciously. "Of course, I didn't think of that. The desire to play and to win is universal, I suppose. But believe me, I shall play better against Mr. Gower if I do it alone."

Benjamin conceded. "I shall go to the village, then follow the path Gower must have taken to see exactly how long it requires, including walking up the bed of the stream."

"You'll freeze!" Antonia exclaimed with concern.

He smiled at her. "Probably. But I'll survive. I'll have a hot bath when I get back. I won't be the only man to get soaked through. Shepherds do it regularly. It's time we did something for Judah, apart from talk, and grieve."

No one argued with him. As he stood up he glanced at Henry. They had not asked him to do anything specific, but the question was in Benjamin's eyes, and Ephraim's also as he rose.

"Oh, I have one or two things to be about," Henry said, excusing himself as they parted in the hallway, he to go upstairs, change into heavier clothes, then head out to the stables to borrow a horse. He was not willing to tell them what he intended. He looked further ahead, and for that he needed to speak to Judah's clerk in his offices in Penrith.

He rode out quickly, hoping not to be seen. He did not wish to be asked his purpose, not yet.

As he climbed the steep road eastward, the wind behind him, he turned it over in his mind. What if Benjamin were to discover that it was not practically possible for Gower to have traveled the distance in the time he had? What if Naomi's questions actually proved Gower's innocence, not of intent, but of being able to have committed the act himself? If they failed to prove Gower's guilt, what lay ahead after that? He wanted to find something, a next step to take, other answers to seek. Was there anyone else Gower could have used, willingly or not? Might there have been an ally in the original case, someone who had not come to light then? Did anyone else profit from that tragedy, or from this?

It was a fine horse, and he found the ride exhilarating, his mind sharper.

There was always the major possibility that in their loathing of Gower and his appalling accusations, they seemed not to have considered whether Judah had other enemies. He had been a judge for some time. There was little enough crime of any seriousness in the Lakes, but it did exist. He must have sentenced other men to fines or imprisonment.

Who else bore him grudges? He did not think for an instant that Judah had been corrupted in anything, but that did not mean that others could not imagine it. Many people refuse to accept that they, or those they love, can be in the wrong, or to blame for their misfortunes. In the short term, it seems easier to blame someone else, to let anger and pride encase you in denial. Some live in it forever. Some accept their own part only when all vengeance has proved futile in healing the flaw that brought them down. The longer you persist in blaming others, the more difficult it becomes to retreat, until finally your whole edifice of belief rests on the lie, and to dismantle it would be self-destruction.

Who else, apart from Gower, might exist in such a self-made prison? He needed to know, just in case the grief and the anger, the lifelong hero worship of an elder brother, had blinded Ephraim and Benjamin to other thoughts.

Henry did not imagine even for an instant that Judah was guilty as Gower accused. He had known Judah well, and loved him as a friend. He had seen him more clearly, having no childhood passions or loyalty of blood. Judah had had faults. He could be overconfident, impatient of those slower of thought than himself. He was omnivorous in his hunger for knowledge, untidy, and he occasionally overshadowed others without realizing it. But he was utterly honest, and as quick to see his own mistakes as anyone else's, and never failed to apologize and amend.

Henry needed to know the truth, all of it. They could not defend Judah, or Antonia, with less.

By the time he arrived he knew exactly what he wanted to do. It took him only a few inquiries at the ostler's where he left the horse, before he was sitting in the office of the court clerk, a James Westwood, who received him with grave courtesy. He sat behind a magnificent walnut desk, his spectacles balanced on the end of his rather long nose.

"I can tell you nothing confidential, you understand," he warned pleasantly.

"Yes, I do understand." Henry nodded. "My son is a barrister in London."

"Rathbone!" Westwood's face lit up. "Really? Oliver Rathbone? Well, well. So he is your son? Fine man." He smiled. "I still can't tell you anything confidential. Not that much of it, mind you. Nasty business. All very foolish."

"The estate was in the Gower family?" Henry began. He repeated essentially what Antonia had told him.

"Precisely," Westwood replied. "Originally the estate was in the Colgrave family. Then Mariah, the widow of Bartram Colgrave. She married Geoffrey Gower and had two sons by him. One of them died as a child, the other is Ashton Gower. But the whole thing was much smaller than before they built that big house, and of course long before they found the archaeological site with all the coins and so on. But I'm ahead of myself." Westwood coughed and cleared his throat. "The widow, Mariah Colgrave, brought not only the land, but a great deal of money to her second marriage. With it Geoffrey Gower purchased more land, and built that house that is the center of the estate now. When he died, it passed to Ashton, his surviving son."

Henry was puzzled. "Then what was it that was forged? And how could Ashton Gower be responsible? It seems to have happened before he was born. How could Peter Colgrave have had any right to it? He wasn't in direct descent."

Westwood pursed his lips. "It's not the estate itself, it's the date of it that's at issue," he explained. "It all hinges on whether the extra part of it, which includes the house, the better part of the land, and the place where the Viking hoard was found, was purchased before Wilbur Colgrave died, or after."

"Who was Wilbur Colgrave?" Rathbone was following it with difficulty.

"Bartram's brother, and Peter Colgrave's father. A matter of which way the inheritance went, you see?" Westwood said. "Before and it should pass to Peter Colgrave, after and it passes to Mariah, and then to her son, Ashton Gower."

"Didn't they know that at the time?" Henry still did not understand. "And if it was a forgery, then

Ashton Gower was not even born, so he couldn't possibly be to blame."

Westwood waved his finger in the air. "Ah, but it was only questioned when Mariah died, just over eleven years ago. Before that everyone took it for granted."

"Well, if Mariah forged it, or Geoffrey did, it is still not Ashton Gower's fault!"

"That is the crux of it!" Westwood said, his face sharp with interest in the problem. "The forgery was recent! They knew that from the ink on the paper, even though whoever did it lifted all the seals off the old one, the family one, and reused them. Very clever, but the rest of it was rubbish!"

"Then why didn't Wilbur Colgrave claim the estate, and the money, at the time? It was rightfully his!" Henry pointed out.

"That is a very good question," Westwood agreed keenly. "He is a bit of a scoundrel, and rumor has it that he was always more than a little in love with Mariah—his brother's wife. By all accounts, she was a real beauty in her day. They even said she paid for the land with personal favors."

He blushed very slightly. "Least said the soonest mended, I think. Anyway, the part that concerns Judah Dreghorn is that when Ashton Gower came to claim his inheritance, Peter Colgrave swore that the Gower deeds to the estate were forged, and it should be his, as heir to Wilbur Colgrave, who was the younger brother and heir to Bartram, rather than his widow, who forfeited it on remarriage. It was entailed, and supposed to remain in the Colgrave name, except that Wilbur died, too, leaving his widow and child, Peter. All rather a mess."

"And Ashton Gower took advantage to try to prove the estate was his by forging a new deed with the right date for Mariah, and thus for him?"

"Precisely," Westwood agreed. "But it failed. The land went back to the Colgrave family, the only one left—Peter. Which was probably where it should have been all the time."

"And Gower went to prison," Henry concluded.

"Quite. It was a great deal of money he attempted to steal by fraud," Westwood said gravely. "It could not go unpunished. The sentence was perfectly fair and appropriate."

"So Ashton Gower lost his home and the fortune he had always assumed to be his. No wonder he was bitter." Henry could imagine it, the young Gower growing up loving the land, riding on it, climbing the hills, feeling he belonged. Then suddenly he lost his father, and his inheritance, the whole nature of his identity and his place in the community was lost. Little wonder he was so angry he could barely think wisely. But it did not excuse dishonesty, and certainly it was not Judah's fault.

"Why did he blame Judah Dreghorn?" he said aloud.

"Ah!" Westwood steepled his fingers. "That is something I don't understand," he admitted. "Gower completely lost control of himself. He ranted and raved at the judge, accusing him of corruption, even at the trial. And then afterwards, when Colgrave sold the estate very quickly, and Dreghorn bought it, Gower swore revenge on Dreghorn for having lied about the whole thing. He said the deeds were genuine, and Dreghorn knew it. Which was all patently ridiculous. But it was extremely ugly. Most distressing."

"And now Judah is dead, in very odd circumstances." Henry looked steadily at Westwood. "Do you believe Gower could be so bent on revenge that he would harm him?"

"Oh, dear." Westwood shook his head a little, obviously distressed. "You are asking me a highly improper question, Mr. Rathbone. It is one I would prefer not to answer. In fact, I really feel that I cannot!" His eyes were very steady, sharp, and bright. His refusal was an answer in itself, and he looked at Henry long enough to make sure that he understood it as such.

"I see." Henry nodded. "Yes, quite plainly. Do you know why Peter Colgrave did not wish to keep the estate?"

"He is another man about whom I prefer not to express an opinion." He smiled very slightly and stared at Henry over the tops of his spectacles. "Don't press

235

me into something that would be indiscreet, and might embarrass us both."

Henry gave a half smile. "Thank you. At least I think I understand something of the actual issues, but not why Ashton Gower imagined he could get away with anything so stupid."

"Arrogance," Westwood said quietly. "I imagine he made the forgery in the heat of anger, perhaps when he discovered the original and realized what it would mean to him. Then he could not back out of it. But that is only my guess."

Henry thanked him and went outside into the cold, already darkening afternoon.

They met before dinner, a little later than usual. Mrs. Hardcastle had prepared a magnificent meal, and the whole house was decorated for Christmas with wreaths of holly, ivy, and pine. There were polished apples and baskets of nuts tied with gold ribbons.

Henry saw it with surprise, in view of the recent, terrible bereavement, and glanced uncertainly at Antonia, in case the servants should have done it without her permission.

She smiled back at him. "It's still Christmas," she said very quietly. "We must not forget or ignore that.

Without Christmas, there would be no hope. And I have to have hope: wild, unreasonable, against all the logic that man can have, things only God can do."

"We all have to," he agreed as they walked into the dining room side by side. "We'll definitely keep Christmas. Thank you."

They took their places and the dishes were served one after another. They were ready for pudding when they finally approached the subject of their achievements during the day.

"I walked all the distances," Benjamin said thoughtfully. "It's possible, but only if you don't hesitate at all. And there would be no time for Gower to have waited for Judah more than five minutes. Not if Judah went straight there. Of course he could have waited for Gower, because we have no idea when he died, except that it was some time before three o'clock when they found him. Also we don't know what time Gower got home again." He turned to Naomi. "Perhaps you do? Did you manage to see him?"

Naomi gave a rueful little shrug. "It was easier than I expected." She looked at Benjamin, avoiding Ephraim's eyes, but both imagined she was perfectly aware that he was looking at her.

"How did you do it?" Antonia asked.

Naomi smiled at her. "With more invention than I am proud to admit," she answered. "Let me do you the favor of not telling you, so you can meet the village with complete innocence. People speak of you so highly." She looked at Antonia with candid regard. "You are much admired, even by those who are stupid enough to listen to Gower. Your reputation is your greatest asset. And when we all go away again, you will remain here and it will matter that it is not changed."

Antonia smiled, but she did not attempt to speak.

Henry had not thought of it in quite those bold terms before, and he realized that perhaps Antonia had not either. None of them had looked beyond the shock and anger of the present. But of course Benjamin would return to the Holy Land. He was probably in the middle of some great excavation. Ephraim would go back again to Africa and his exploration, the plants and discoveries that so fascinated him. Naomi would make the long journey back to America, and then westward once more to take up Nathaniel's work, and her own friends in the life they had made there. Even Henry would return to Primrose Hill, and the joys and cares of London. Antonia would then taste the full measure of her loneliness.

Henry remembered the death of his own wife. At first, shock numbs much of the deepest ache. There are things that have to be done, people told, arrangements made. One forces courage to surmount weakness and for the sake of other people, one behaves with dignity.

But afterward, when the first mourning is over and

the attention goes, friends and family return to their own lives, then the true weight of loss descends. Everything one used to share is no longer as it was. The silence of the heart is deafening. Antonia had yet to face that.

Naomi had already experienced it, but she at least had some work that would occupy her energies and her thoughts. Of course Antonia had the estate to run, and her care for Joshua, but his grief was her burden as well.

"What did you learn?" Benjamin was asking Naomi now. She had already answered some of his questions, and Henry had not been listening.

"He seems to have spent the evening with the Pilkingtons," Naomi replied, a faint look of distaste on her face. "Mrs. Pilkington is a woman of extraordinarily generous bosom, balanced by an opposingly mean spirit. She has opinions as to the moral value of everything, good or bad. *Decadent* is her favorite word. I don't know why, because I don't think she knows what it means."

"She is new money?" Henry inquired, aware of all the social differences that carried, the envy and the ambition.

Naomi's face lit with a smile, broad and candid. "Exactly! Old money must be immorally obtained. Hers is new, of course. She has espoused Gower's cause, precisely because the older families can't stand him. And the violin recital was 'decadent,' so she did not attend. She probably doesn't know Bach from Mozart, and doesn't want to be upstaged, poor soul." There was a sudden thread of pity in her voice, as if the absurdity of pretension had betrayed its inner fear and its emptiness.

Ephraim saw it, and a shred of its meaning registered as surprise on his face, not at the village, but at what he had glimpsed in Naomi, a new beauty. "But Gower was there?" He grasped at the personal meaning.

"Yes. He left to go home at just after ten," she replied.

"Then he could have got to the lower crossing by the time Judah did," Benjamin deduced. "But it would have been hard. Don't the Pilkingtons live right down by the water?"

"Yes."

He thought for a moment. "He would have to have had luck on his side," he said. "Or else Judah stood around for some time waiting for him. I asked everyone I could about that day, the servants here, the post office and in the village. There's no word of anyone delivering a message to Judah to meet Gower, or one from Judah to him. And it's not a place anyone would meet by chance."

"Frankly, it's not a place anyone would meet at all," Henry said. "I still find it hard to accept."

"We have to," Benjamin argued. "That's where

Judah was, or he couldn't have found the knife. And the higher crossing is just as absurd, but that's where he was found." He turned to Naomi. "What did you think of Gower?"

She hesitated. "A very angry man, one who hits out first, in case he doesn't get a later chance," she replied. "A man so filled with his own emotions he doesn't have time or room to consider anyone else's. I'm not sure that I wanted to see any good in him, but if there was any, it was easy to overlook. But he is far from a fool. Which is why I wonder how he ever thought he could get away with such a stupid forgery."

"Even the most intelligent people can behave idiotically once in a while when their passions are in control," Henry said, pursing his lips as memory stabbed him. "We lose peripheral vision and see only what we want. It's a sort of mental arrogance. Being intelligent is not always the same thing as being wise—or honest."

Naomi looked at him and the warmth of her smile was as if the fire had suddenly burned up, dispelling the shadows and the cold places in the room.

"No, it isn't," she agreed. "But they are the things most worth winning, and without them the rest is of little value. I should be more sorry for Ashton Gower, and for stupid Mrs. Pilkington. It's themselves they are cheating in the end."

Ephraim sat very quiet, almost without moving.

One needed to look at him carefully to realize how fully his concentration was on Naomi.

"Could he have killed Judah? Is it possible?" Benjamin asked softly.

Ephraim turned to him. "Yes," he answered. "And I can't like Colgrave, he's a cold man, for all that he hides it, but he'll help us, at least in this. He hates the injustice, for us and for the whole village. It's bad for everyone."

Benjamin nodded. "Good. We have made a start, but it is not proof."

"What else can we do?" Antonia asked. She was troubled, trying hard to hide the desperation inside her. She was beginning to face the long future ahead after they had gone and she was alone in the village, the whispers, the thoughts, her dead husband's memory to protect and her son to nurture, and keep his faith and certainty strong.

Benjamin looked at her. "I don't know yet. But we will succeed. Judah was our brother, and I, at least, will never leave here until I have cleared his name, I promise!"

"Nor will I," Ephraim said fiercely. "I give you my word, for you, for Joshua, and for Judah himself."

She bent her head, the tears spilling over her cheeks. "Thank you."

*T*he morning was sharp with high, drifting clouds and a thin sunshine. Henry rose early, had a cup of tea, and then dressed and went out. He preferred to walk alone and think. They had spoken brave words the evening before, but they had no plans that were assured of giving them the proof they needed. They were loyal, that was never in question. They were brave. Benjamin had the logic and the acute intelligence to marshal all the information they could acquire, and the force of mind to present it. Ephraim had the strength to face whatever unpleasantness, difficulty, or obstruction the people in the village might use, or to face Ashton Gower himself. Nothing would cause him to retreat from what he believed to be right, no matter what the cost.

And Naomi had a charm and wit, an imagination to understand others, a warmth to disarm them, so she could glean all kinds of information that a more direct, confrontational approach would not. Henry found himself liking her more with each encounter. He could easily see why Ephraim had fallen in love with her, and remained so even over the years since she had left. In fact it was less easy to understand why Benjamin had not!

Why had she chosen the quieter, far less dynamic Nathaniel? That was something Henry felt he would never understand. But then what man ever really understands the choices of women?

He walked rapidly westward along the way Judah had gone on the night of his death. Apparently it was the easiest way from the house to the site of the Viking hoard, and he had not yet seen it. The air was crisp and sweet, and he saw wild birds wheeling in the sky and only a little higher on the slopes of the hills, the dark forms of deer grazing. A winter-coated hare loped across the snow only twenty yards away. He thought how infinitely more beautiful this was than the dripping, smoke-darkened streets of London, or of any other city.

He crossed the stream over the narrow stone bridge, balancing with great care, although there was not actually ice on it, as he was much relieved to find.

Then instead of going toward the church, he turned upstream and followed the path where it had led along the bank, and then climbed away. There was a small wooden notice indicating that he was almost there.

He saw it as soon as he breasted the rise, its remaining walls etched dark against the snow. Behind it a lone man stood staring across the wind-rippled water, which was blue and silver and gray. He knew who it was before his footsteps crunching on the snow made him turn: Ashton Gower, bare-headed, his black hair and fierce eyes making him look as if he belonged to the landscape, even to the period when this shrine had been built. It gave Henry an odd feeling of intrusion, as if he were trying to alter history to make his own people belong in someone else's heritage.

He dismissed it with irritation. It was a trick of the light and his imagination. "Good morning, Mr. Gower," he said politely. He considered saying something agreeable about the view, or even the possibility of more snow blowing up from beyond Helvellyn, and changed his mind. It would make him sound as if he were nervous. He did not mean it, and they both knew that.

Gower swept his arm wide. "Like it?" he asked. "I'd welcome you to my land, but the law has taken it from me. You can come here any time you want, if the Dreghorns say you can. I can come here only to the point open to the public. But I refuse to pay!"

"Has anyone asked you to?" Henry inquired, standing beside him and looking at the water, the mountains, and the sky, wild, wind-ragged, ever-shifting patterns of light and shadow.

"Not yet," Gower replied. "Even Dreghorn hadn't the nerve to do that. He knew he was wrong, you know? He couldn't look me in the eye. More grace than his brothers." His mouth twisted. "Or more guilt!"

"I've known Judah Dreghorn for twenty years," Henry told him levelly, controlling his temper with difficulty. "Apart from what I know, there's no one else who has an ill word to say of him. I also know what they say of you, Mr. Gower, and it is far less flat-

245

tering. I assume you are claiming that the expert in forgery was lying as well? Why? Are you so hated here that men will perjure their souls to see you punished for something you did not do? Why? What have you done to earn that?"

Gower shivered, hunching his shoulders as if the wind were suddenly blowing off ice. "The deeds I got from my father's safe were genuine," he said, facing Henry directly. "I can't prove that, but they were. The land was his. Wilbur Colgrave might have been in love with my mother, but no Colgrave yielded his land for anyone. The reason he didn't claim it was that he had no right to. That whole story of an affair was a slander. But who can prove that now?" There was pain in his voice, deep and angry, but so real Henry could feel it tear inside him also. Perhaps it was for his mother's reputation as much as for himself. Henry would find it unbearable were such a thing suggested of his mother.

How much can pain justify? Did Colgrave have to have revealed that very private detail? Could he not at least have kept that much silent? There was an unspoken understanding that one did not blacken the names of the dead who could no longer speak for themselves!

But then that was exactly what Gower was doing to Judah. Henry said as much aloud.

Gower turned to stare at him, confusion and frustration in his face. "How else can I defend myself?"

he demanded, his voice almost choking. "This land is mine! They took my home, my heritage, my mother's good name, and mine! And made me pay for it with eleven years of my life, while they took the spoils. Now I'm a branded man, without a roof over my head except I labor for it, and pay week by week. I'm supposed to accept that? That's your idea of justice, the Dreghorn way?"

"And the forged deeds?" Henry asked. "Or did the expert lie? Why? Is Judah Dreghorn supposed to have paid them, too?"

"I don't know. I do know the document I gave them was genuine, and it said the land was my father's. The dates were right." There was no doubt in Gower's face, no flicker, only blind, furious certainty.

There was no answer. Henry turned away and walked back to the house. He went straight to the stable, requested a horse, and rode out along the road to Penrith. He needed to know the exact history of where the deeds had been kept from the time of Geoffrey Gower's death until the expert from Kendal had examined them and pronounced them to be forged. Doubt was gnawing at his mind, shapeless, uncertain, but fraying the edges of all his thoughts. He did not doubt Judah's honesty, but could he have been mistaken, perhaps duped by someone else? It was a disturbing idea, but Henry could not leave it unanswered.

The town was busy with the usual trade and market. The streets were crowded with people coming and going. Wagons were piled with bales of woolen cloth. All the traditional manufactures of the Lakes were there: clogs, slate, bobbins, iron goods, pottery, pencils. And every kind of food: oats, mutton, fresh fish, especially salmon, potatoes, Forty Shilling and Keswick Codling apples, and spices from the coast.

Henry pushed his way through and eventually found himself at Judah's offices again. It was a long, tedious task to trace the arrival of the deed and its exact whereabouts from that time forward until it was taken to be shown to the specialist in Kendal.

"Ah, yes," the junior clerk said knowingly. "Very sad. Never suspected Mr. Dreghorn of anything like that, I must say. Goes to show."

Henry froze, anger built up inside him. "Goes to show what, Mr. Johnson?" he said coldly. "That memories are short and loyalty thin?" Then the instant he had said it he regretted his lack of self-control. He was making his own task harder.

Johnson flushed scarlet. "I don't believe them!" he protested. "You do me wrong to think I did, sir, and that's a fact."

Henry shifted his own position, perhaps a little less than honestly. He had assumed the man was speaking for himself. There had been no outrage in his face. "I was referring to those who do, whoever they are," he amended. "I trust that having known Mr. Dreghorn you would be the last to agree, and the first to defend him."

"Of course I would," Johnson said with a sniff.

Henry used his advantage. "Then I am sure you will be as eager as I am to clear it up beyond question. I need to follow the history of those deeds that were sworn to be forgeries. When did they come here? Who brought them and from where? Where were they kept? Who had access to them, and who took them to Kendal to show to . . . what is his name?"

"Mr. Percival, sir."

"Yes. Good. If anyone did tamper with them, it was not Mr. Dreghorn." He made it a statement that could not be argued with.

"Of course it wasn't!" Johnson agreed truculently.

But it was a slower task than Henry had expected, and Johnson was, above all, protective of his own reputation. He now had a new master and was determined to appear in the right. Judah was gone and could be of no more help.

Henry caught him in a couple of self-serving lies before he was certain beyond argument as to the history of the deeds. The matter had taken well over a week, and during that time no one had looked at them. Undeniably, Judah could have altered them, or replaced them with forgeries. But so could a number of other people with either access to the office, or to the messenger who had carried them to Kendal. And of course it still left the time they had been in Mr. Percival's care, a further two weeks or more. All were unlikely, but none was impossible.

Henry thanked Johnson, who was now a good deal more anxious, then returned to the stable where he had left his horse, and set out on the long ride back to the estate.

He turned the problem over in his mind all the way. Who had had the time, the opportunity, and the skill to make the forgery? The paper had apparently been wrong, and the ink, so they were easy enough to come by. The old seals had been removed from the original deeds, and glued back on the new ones. Time seemed to be the major element. But they had been in Judah's offices for a week, then transported to Kendal and in Percival's office for another two weeks. For anyone familiar with the deeds, it would take only a day to take them, create the forgery, destroy the original, and put the forgery back.

It might be more difficult to prove who had actually done it. Unfortunately Judah was the person with the best opportunity, apart from Mr. Percival, of course. But there was no reason to suppose he had any interest in the matter.

Henry continued to think about it as he rode. He found the stark beauty of the winter landscape peculiarly comforting. Its clean lines, wind-scoured, had a kind of courage about it, as if it had endured all that the violence of nature could heap on it, and pretension was swept away. The cold air stung his face, but his horse was a willing and agreeable animal, and there was a companionship in their journey. He thanked it with affection when he finally dismounted in the stable yard and went into the house.

The evening was much more difficult. No one else had learned anything they felt to be of use. The whispers in the village were growing louder and each of them had heard remarks which at the best could be regarded as doubting, beginning to question whether Judah was actually as honest as he had seemed. Other cases were recalled where people had protested their innocence, even though a jury had found them guilty. There was no direct accusation, nothing specific to deny or disprove, just an unpleasantness in the air.

Henry said that he had been to Penrith. He did not want to make a secret of it or it might seem underhanded, and anyway the groom would know because of the horse. But he did not tell anyone why he had gone, or precisely where.

They sat around the dinner table with another delicious meal. Mrs. Hardcastle had made one of the local delicacies for pudding—a dish known as rum nicky—made of rum, brown sugar, dried fruit, and Cumberland apples.

Antonia spoke because it was her home and they were her guests. She would not allow them to sit uncomfortably in silence, but it was all trivia, little bits of news about sheep dog trials last summer, boat races on the lake, who had climbed which mountain, what weather to expect.

Henry was aware of Ephraim one moment looking at Naomi, the next carefully avoiding her eyes. Whatever it was that he felt for her, she did not wish to acknowledge it, and yet Henry was absolutely certain that she knew.

And all the time at the back of his mind was the fear that they would all have to be told the possibility that in some way, through misplaced trust, inattention, some kind of carelessness, Judah had made an error, and Gower was not guilty of forging the deeds, which must mean that someone else was.

Who else profited? Peter Colgrave, that was obvious. Had anyone else thought they could buy the estate cheaply? Had anyone known of the Viking hoard, with its gold and silver coins, its jewelry and artifacts, not to mention its historic value? That was another thing to find out, if possible.

But sitting at the table, seeing their faces, the tension, the anger, and the grief, he dared not approach it yet. But how long could he wait?

After the meal was finished Antonia went upstairs to say good night to Joshua, and Henry knew from the evenings before that she would be gone for quite a long time, perhaps an hour or more. Joshua was nine years old, still a child in his hurt and confusion, trying hard to earn the respect of his uncles, to behave like the man he thought they expected him to be.

And he was also intelligent enough to know that

they were protecting him from something else. Henry had seen his face as they changed the subject when he came in while they were speaking of Gower, or the village. They did not know children. They did not realize how much he heard, how quick he was to catch an evasion, a note of unintended patronage. He could see fear, even if he could not give it a name.

Henry could remember how Oliver had constantly surprised him with his grasp of things Henry had assumed to be beyond him. He watched, he copied, he understood. Joshua Dreghorn was just as eager and as quick. Antonia knew that, and she was spending her time, and perhaps her emotions, with him.

Henry invited Naomi to accompany him for a short walk in the starlit garden, which she accepted. He held her cloak for her, then put on his own coat, and led the way to the side door.

"What is it?" she asked as soon as they were a couple of yards from the house. "Have you learned something?"

There was no time to approach it obliquely. "I went to see a clerk in Judah's office in Penrith," he answered. "I asked him exactly where the deeds had been since they were taken out of Geoffrey Gower's safe." He spoke quietly, although the crunch of their footsteps on the frost-hardened grass might well have disguised their voices, had anyone near an open window been listening. "There was time and opportunity

for someone to have altered it . . . changed it for another."

"You mean put a forgery in place of a genuine
one?" She saw what he meant immediately, and there
was fear in her voice. With the hood of her cloak up
he could see little of her face.

"Yes," he replied.

"You believe Gower?" It was a direct question,
filled with incredulity, but asked nonetheless.

He could not answer immediately, not with complete honesty.

"Mr. Rathbone?" she demanded, gripping his arm
and pulling him to a stop.

"I don't believe Judah would have done such a
thing, for any reason whatever," he said unhesitat-
ingly. Of that he was absolutely sure. "But he may
have trusted people he should not have."

Her voice was very low. "Have you told that to
anyone else?"

"No." He was smiling in the dark, but it was self-
mockery, there was no pleasure in it at all. "I have
spent all my ride back from Penrith and a good deal
of the evening trying not to do so. But it is a possibility we have to face."

"You are sure there was opportunity?"

"Yes."

"Who? If not Gower, why would anyone else? He
was the only one who would profit from such a stupid forgery!"

They started to walk again, heading farther away from the house, and anyone who might look out and see them.

"He made the date into the one that would mean the property was his!" she went on, still holding his arm. "The other date would have left it as Peter Colgrave's, as it was. Then we bought it. No one else had anything to gain from changing it."

"There is no answer that fits the facts," he told her. "Ashton Gower swears that the deeds were not forged, the expert says that they were. The forged date favors Gower."

"Yes. Isn't that proof?"

The thought he had been fighting against all day crystalized in his mind.

"What if the forgery is not a change at all?"

"But that makes no . . ." She stopped. "Oh, no! You mean if the forgery is an exact copy of the original, date included? So Gower was telling the truth when he said the deed was genuine? Then it was replaced by an obvious forgery, with exactly the same date, so Gower would be disbelieved—lose his land!"

"Yes."

"That is terrible! But who? Colgrave?"

"Perhaps. Or anyone else who thought they might be able to buy the estate cheaply."

"Judah bought it from Colgrave, at the price he asked. He was in a hurry for the money. I think he

255

had debts. Maybe someone else expected to buy, and didn't get the chance. That could be anyone!"

"Maybe someone else had already found the Viking hoard and knew what it would be worth," Henry pointed out. "Colgrave didn't, or he would have asked a far larger sum."

"And Gower believes it was Judah." Her voice was somber and tight with strain. "Perhaps he really didn't do it, is that possible? Without knowing it, Judah sent an innocent man to prison!"

"Yes, it is possible." He loathed admitting it. "Of course it is also possible that he is as guilty as sin of killing Judah," he added. "Somebody did. No one else we know had a reason—except the real forger."

"Perhaps Gower has enemies, too?" she suggested. "He's a most disagreeable man. Is it possible he is the real intended victim, and Judah is only the means they use?"

"Yes, of course it is. And I don't know where we would even begin to look for them!"

She bent her head. "This is terrible!" she said in a whisper. "We have to know! Don't we?"

"I think so. Could you rest with it unanswered?"

"I don't know. It doesn't matter for me. When it's over, when we've silenced Gower, I'll go back to America again. I have the excitement, the discovery, the sheer blazing beauty of it. There is a magic to the unknown like nothing else." Her voice was filled with vitality.

It reminded Henry of Ephraim when he had spoken of Africa and the wild beauty of that country, too. Again he wondered why Naomi had chosen the safer Nathaniel with his softer ways.

"Do you miss it?" he asked aloud.

"I've been too busy to, so far," she said honestly.

"We will have to tell them the possibility that the deeds were changed," he said as they came to the end of the lawn and looked across at the glimmering light on the lake, visible only as movement, like black silk in the wind.

"I know. Antonia will be terribly hurt, as if we have suddenly abandoned her." She sighed. "Benjamin will be confused, but I think he can't be utterly shocked. He's too clever not to have thought of it, even if only to deny it."

"And Ephraim?" he asked, knowing she would find that the hardest to answer.

She hesitated before she spoke. "He'll be angry. He'll think we have betrayed Judah. He doesn't forgive easily."

Henry looked at her, the little of her face he could see in the starlight, but all he could glean from her was the emotion he heard in her voice. Was it in general she thought Ephraim did not forgive, or was there some specific sin she spoke of? Had Nathaniel really been her first choice, or was he second, and she would not now make a decision, even for her own

257

happiness, which she felt betrayed him? She had used the word herself, referring to Ephraim's emotions.

He asked, even though it was intrusive. "You speak as if you know him well, and I can't help seeing his feelings for you."

She smiled. "You are wondering why I married Nathaniel, when Ephraim also asked me?"

"Yes," he admitted.

"Because love is more than passion and excitement, Mr. Rathbone. If you trust your life and your love to someone, you need to admire their courage, and Ephraim has any amount of that. But if you are going to live with them every day, not just the good ones, but the bad ones as well, the difficult ones when you fail, make mistakes, feel bruised and afraid, you need to be certain of their kindness. You need someone who will forgive you when you are wrong, because you will be wrong sometimes."

He did not interrupt. They stood side by side looking toward the water. It was cold and very clear, the stars tiny, glittering shards of light in the enormity of space.

"Ephraim has not been wrong often enough to understand," she said almost under her breath.

"It seems to me you are not wrong very often, either," he observed. "And yet you have a gentleness."

This time he saw her smile. "I have been. I look like my mother. She behaved badly. I never knew why, but

I imagine sometimes how lonely she might have felt, or what made her do as she did. My father never forgave her for it, so even if she had wished to return her heart to him, he did not allow her to."

He pictured another woman like Naomi, perhaps bored with nothing on which to use her intelligence, no adventure to take her from the domestic round, and possibly loved more for her beauty than for her inner self. How deeply had her unhappiness marked her daughter that she chose the gentleness of a forgiving man rather than the passion of one she feared might repeat her parents' history?

"I see," he said very gently. "Of course you did. We all need to be forgiven, one time or another. And we need to talk, to share our own dreams, as well as those of the one we love."

She reached up very gently and kissed his cheek. "I always liked Nathaniel, and I learned to love him. I loved Ephraim from the beginning, but I don't trust him to forgive my mistakes, and forget them, and to hold my heart softly."

For a moment or two he did not speak. When he did, it was of the problem they shared, now a burden growing heavier by the minute.

"I think I shall go to Kendal tomorrow and see the expert who testified about the deeds." He turned to face her. "Then I have to tell Benjamin and Ephraim what I find, and I suppose if it is irrefutable, Antonia, too."

"Do you think Ashton Gower was imprisoned falsely?" she asked.

"I think that it is possible, and if it is true, then we must acknowledge it and try to redress as much of the injustice as may be reached now."

"But somebody killed Judah!" she protested. "His body did not wash upstream! And if Gower really was innocent, does that not give him the most intense reason to seek revenge? Perhaps he didn't mean to kill Judah, it was just a fight that ended when Judah slipped and fell, and for some reason Gower dragged his body all the way up to the higher crossing. But why would he do that?"

"Maybe at the time of Judah's death there were some signs in the snow that another person had been there, and even of the struggle," Henry reasoned. "He could not afford to have it investigated, or at that time it might have been easy enough to show he was there, too. And with their history, who would believe him that it was accidental?"

"I think he is a loathsome man," she said, beginning to walk slowly back toward the house. "But I am sorry for him. If it really was an accident, then if we could help him prove it, we ought to—oughtn't we?"

"Yes." He had no doubt.

"The family won't like that." There was certainty in her voice, too, and fear. She wanted to belong. She had loved them all since she had first known them.

They were the only family she had. Like Antonia, she was otherwise alone.

"We don't know yet," he pointed out. "At least not beyond doubt. I'll go to Kendal tomorrow."

And with that they walked back up the grass and in through the door again to the warmth.

PART THREE

*I*N THE MORNING HENRY RODE EARLY TO PENRITH, and took the train to Kendal, which was the next stop on the way south toward Lancaster. He was in the town by half past ten, and found the office of the expert in forged documents, Mr. Percival. He was younger than Henry had expected, perhaps no more than in his middle thirties. He was clean shaven, with a thick head of reddish-brown hair, and an agreeable expression as he showed Henry into his office.

The pleasure in his face faded rather rapidly when Henry explained the area of his interest.

"Yes, I heard that Gower was making accusations," Percival said drily. "A great shame. A most unpleasant man, and completely irresponsible. A tragedy that Dreghorn should die in a wretched accident like that. However, I don't think that there is anything I can do to assist you, Mr. Rathbone." He leaned back a little with a slight smile. "You need a solicitor. Such slanderous talk should be addressed by the law. I am sure Mrs. Dreghorn already has someone who represents the family, but if you need anyone further, I can recommend someone easily enough."

"Thank you, but that is not necessary." Henry reminded himself that this man was a forgery expert, a witness in court, but not a lawyer of any kind. Nothing that he said to him was he obliged to keep in confidence. "I am interested in learning more of precisely what happened. I think that is a far better defense than legal restriction, and certainly swifter and more honest than suits for slander, which may drag on and become most unpleasant."

Percival leaned back in his chair and bit his lower lip. "The truth, Mr. Rathbone, is that the deeds to the estate owned by Geoffrey Gower and bequeathed to his son, Ashton Gower, were actually forgeries, and not very good ones. That has been established at law, and Ashton Gower sentenced to prison for his part in it."

"How do we know that it was Ashton Gower who forged them, and not his father?" Henry asked with an air of innocence.

Percival smiled patiently. "Because in earlier sight of them, during previous transactions, they were never questioned. And frankly, Mr. Rathbone, the forgeries were extremely poor. No one used to dealing in legal documents of any sort would have been fooled by them."

"And yet you did not immediately report the fact that they were forged," Henry pointed out. "At first glance, you noticed nothing amiss."

Percival colored uncomfortably. "I looked only at certain parts of them, Mr. Rathbone, I confess to that. The first reading of them in their entirety showed us the falsity of them. There is no question. Frankly I am not sure what it is you are trying to prove. Gower is a forger. Judah Dreghorn had no choice but to sentence him to imprisonment. Everything else is spurious, just a weak and vicious man making excuses for himself."

"You have a deep personal dislike for Gower, Mr. Percival," Henry observed.

Percival's face tightened. "I do. And I am far from alone, Mr. Rathbone. He is a most objectionable man, without the grace or the honesty to repent of his crime, nor the courage to begin again and attempt to live a decent life. Instead of that, which might earn him forgiveness, he has attempted to blacken the name of an honest judge who did no more than his duty. If you had known Judah Dreghorn, you would understand my anger."

"I did know him," Henry said, keeping his voice calm only with an effort. "He was my friend for over twenty years. Mrs. Dreghorn is my goddaughter. That does not address the question of who forged the document, and when."

"For heaven's sake, man!" Percival snapped. "Ashton Gower forged it at some point between the original being taken from his father's safe, and this forgery produced to justify his claim to the estate!" Percival snapped.

"You are an expert in forgery?"

"I am!"

"So it would be brought to you for that purpose, but not until forgery was suspected?"

"Of course."

"Who saw it first, prior to that?"

"William Overton, a solicitor."

"Did he testify in the case?" Henry asked.

"No."

"Why not?"

"He was not called. Why should he be? No one claimed that the deeds were genuine, except Gower himself, and he was obviously lying. As I said, Mr. Rathbone, the work was shoddy to a degree. Any examination of them made the fact plain. Now, if you don't mind, I have other clients to see, to whom I may be of more service. I am afraid I cannot help you, and to be candid, I have no desire to. You seem to be defending a man who has maligned a judge we all admired, and who apparently considered you to be a friend."

Henry remained sitting. "When is it supposed that Gower forged the deeds, Mr. Percival?"

Percival was barely patient. "Before he brought them to his solicitor, sir! When else?"

"Mr. Overton?"

"Precisely."

"They passed from him to Mr. Overton, to you?"

Percival hesitated, his face a trifle flushed. "No, not exactly. They were questioned by Colgrave, and he demanded sight of them, which happened in Judge Dreghorn's office, I believe."

"Why not in Mr. Overton's? Was he not the Gowers' solicitor?"

"Mr. Colgrave required that it be before a judge, and Mr. Overton was perfectly satisfied that it be so. I really don't understand what it is you are trying to prove, Mr. Rathbone!" Percival said irritably.

"I am trying to see when they might have been tampered with, that Mr. Gower could sustain an accusation that Judah Dreghorn, or anyone but himself, could have forged them," Henry replied.

"For heaven's sake, man! You don't believe him!" Percival was aghast.

"I am trying to prove Judah Dreghorn's innocence," Henry answered. "If he never had them in his possession, then he must be!"

"Well . . . well, his reputation is sufficient. The deeds were in several different people's possession, if you wish to be legal about it. It would be far better, and wiser, if you were to allow the matter to drop. No one will believe Gower. The man is already a convicted criminal."

"Yes," Henry agreed. He rose to his feet. "Where may I find this Mr. Overton?"

"In the offices at the end of the street. I do not know the number."

"Thank you. Good day, Mr. Percival."

Percival did not reply.

Henry walked as directed, and found the offices of William Overton after the briefest of questions. He was obliged to wait only twenty minutes in order to see him.

"Come in, Mr. Rathbone," Overton said with courtesy. He was older than Percival. What there was of his hair was gray, almost white, but his lean face was only slightly lined and he moved with ease. "My clerk says that you are concerned about the deeds that were forged regarding the Gower estate. Terrible tragedy that Judah Dreghorn drowned. I am most deeply sorry. A charming man, of the utmost honesty. What may I do for you?" He waved at the chair opposite his desk, and resumed his own seat.

Henry sat down and told him as briefly as he could.

Overton frowned. "I am not an expert in forgery, Mr. Rathbone. I admit that the document seemed genuine to me, and I have handled a good many in the course of my profession."

"What was the date on the original document that you had from Geoffrey Gower's safe, compared with the document presented in court, which Mr. Percival testified to as forged?"

"They were the same, Mr. Rathbone," Overton replied, frowning. "That is why I do not understand the claim that the deeds presented at court were forged."

"The dates were the same?" Henry swallowed hard. "You are certain?"

"Of course I am certain."

"Then what was the purpose of the forgery?"

"I don't know. But most certainly it was not to gain the estate for Ashton Gower. It was his anyway." Overton leaned forward across his desk. His face was sad and touched with a deep distress. "It seems to me that someone changed a true document for a false one, but it read exactly the same. The only purpose in that would have been to discredit the genuine deeds. That possibility does not seem to have occurred to anyone at the trial."

"When were you aware of this, Mr. Overton?" Henry was puzzled. Why had this apparently honest man not spoken of what seemed to be a monstrous miscarriage of justice?

"Just over two weeks ago, on the day of Judah Dreghorn's death, he came to me with just the questions you have asked . . ."

Henry felt as if he had been struck a physical blow. Ashton Gower was innocent, and Judah had known it! Why, then, would Gower have killed him?

Or was it not Gower at all, but someone else?

He heard Overton's voice as if from a long way off—words garbled and making no sense.

271

"I beg your pardon?" he said numbly. "I'm afraid I did not hear you."

"You look ill, Mr. Rathbone," Overton repeated. "May I pour you a glass of brandy? I am afraid this has come as a great shock to you." He suited his actions to his words, rising to open a cupboard and pour a fairly stiff measure of very good brandy into a glass, and place it on the edge of the desk where Henry could reach it.

"Thank you." Henry took it and drank it slowly. He felt its fire inside him and was grateful, but it did not take away the knowledge that filled him with horror.

"Judah was here, and you told him what you told me?" He knew he must sound foolish, but he could not grasp the idea of it.

"Yes," Overton agreed. "And he was as horrified as you are. He realized what had happened . . . what he had done, if you like, albeit in complete innocence."

"Did he . . ." Henry swallowed. "Did he say what he intended to do?"

Overton smiled, a small, unhappy gesture full of pity. "Not precisely. He left here quite early in the afternoon. I think he took the half past two train to Penrith. He said he intended to see someone, but he did not say who, nor what he meant to say to them. He would have been in Penrith before half past three, and perhaps home by five, if he had a good horse. He wished to go to a recital in the village where he lives. It was something to do with his son, who I understand is remarkably gifted."

"Yes. Yes, he is." Henry was still thinking in a daze. He tried to imagine what must have been in Judah's mind as he traveled home that day. He knew that Ashton Gower had been innocent. Was it Gower he had intended to see? Or someone else—someone who was guilty?

Had he been too late to see them before the recital? He would not miss it and disappoint Joshua. Had he planned to see that person after his return home, at the lower crossing? Why there? Closer to the village, but yet private? Closer to the church? The Viking site? Colgrave's house? Or halfway between the estate and someone else's house?

Who was it, and what had transpired? If it was Gower, then had Judah's death been the tragic and idiotic result of an explosion of rage at the injustice of the eleven years Gower had spent in prison for a crime he had not committed?

That was possible.

It was equally possible that it was not Ashton Gower at all, but someone else. Peter Colgrave? Or someone who had intended to buy the estate, and been prevented?

One thing was certain: Henry could not leave the matter secret now. The injustice burned like a fire inside him, demanding reparation. If he permitted Ashton Gower to carry the shame of the first crime, and then the fear of the stigma for the second, he would be more guilty than Gower could ever be, because he knew the truth.

"Why did you not do something when you heard of Judah's death, and knew he could not right it?" he asked Overton.

"My dear Rathbone, I have no proof!" Overton replied, turning up his hands. "I saw the original deed, but it is destroyed now. Only the forgery remains. What could I say, and to whom? Judah Dreghorn could have, but he is dead."

Of course. Henry should have seen it. Again he felt as if the ground had risen up and struck him, bruising him bone deep. It rested with him. There was no one else.

Slowly and a trifle shakily, he rose to his feet, thanked Overton, and made his way back to the station. He sat in the train all the way to Penrith thinking about it, mulling over anything and everything he could say to the family. None of it stopped the pain in the least, and none of it would be acceptable to them, or dull their anger with him.

He arrived at the house just in time for dinner. It was one of the most miserable of his life. The food was rich, succulent, as if preparing for the taste for the Christmas goose and all the added fare of the season, but it might have been so much stale bread, for any pleasure it gave him.

"We are accomplishing nothing!" Benjamin said miserably. "Gower is still blackening Judah's name. I heard more of it today and I don't see how we can stop him, except by going to law. Antonia?"

She looked sad and frightened. Henry knew her thoughts were even more of Joshua than for herself. Like any woman who had a child, her will, her emotions, her instinct were all to protect him. She must hurt for Judah also, but her first thought would be for the living. She would perhaps do her real mourning after he was safe.

"If it has to be," she conceded, but Henry heard the reluctance in her voice, and she turned to him for confirmation that this was the only course.

He hesitated. He would have to tell her the truth, but he dreaded it, and he had not the words yet.

Naomi also looked at Henry, but in her eyes was the question formed by knowledge he had been to Kendal today. He had not told her, he had had no opportunity to speak to her alone, but in that glance she understood. Would she have the courage to risk the love of the family, and help him?

Ephraim filled the silence. "Only if there's no other way," he said grimly. "We won't leave until we've cleared Judah's name from this stupid charge, and proved to everyone that Gower killed him. Then he'll be hanged, and no one will ever repeat anything he said." He looked at Antonia with a sudden gentleness. "He was our brother, we'll see justice for his

sake. But you are as much a part of our family, and
Joshua is the only Dreghorn of the next generation.
We would never leave you unprotected." That was
his way of saying that he loved them. Such plain,
emotional words were not in his nature.

"Thank you," Antonia said warmly. "I know how
eager you are to return to your work, and to the marvelous places you travel."

Benjamin smiled. "When I go back to Palestine
we're going to be working in the streets of Jerusalem.
We're tracing the way Christ took on Palm Sunday,
when he entered in triumph." His face was lit with a
fire that had nothing to do with the chandelier above
the table. His mind saw the far-off glory of a different
and deeper kind, and for a moment all anger was forgotten. The fire of his emotion burned away lesser,
worldly griefs. "Next we are going to find and make
certain of the garden where Mary Magdalene spoke
to the risen Christ on Easter Sunday. Can you imagine? We will stand where she stood when He said
'Mary,' and she knew Him!"

"Perhaps that is where we are all trying to stand,"
Naomi said very quietly. "Only I'm not sure it is a
place, I think it is a matter of spirit, it is who you have
become."

There was another long moment's silence.

"But it must be wonderful for you to see it, of
course," she added, as if not to spoil his excitement.
She turned to Ephraim. "Where will you go next?"

He smiled very slightly—an inward pleasure. "The Rift Valley, in South Africa," he answered. "The plants there are different from anywhere else on earth. I expect to see some wonderful animals, too, but I shan't be studying them. We could find new foods, new medicines, and of course the beauty of them is staggering, shapes and colors you never see here." His voice warmed and became more urgent, and without realizing it he was using his hands to echo the shapes he envisioned. "The variety of creation amazes me more and more every day. It's not just the endless invention of it, it's how every design has unique and absolute purpose! You know . . ." He stopped, realizing with a moment of self-consciousness how his love of it had swept him along. "Another time," he finished. "When we have dealt with Gower."

Again Henry tried to think how to begin what he must tell them, and his nerve failed. How blunt should he be? How immediate, or how gentle?

Ephraim had asked Naomi where she was planning to go, and his face was tense, as if he too were struggling with inner turmoil as to what he should say, and how. He feared another rejection. Henry could see that in the tight angles of Ephraim's body, as he sat at the foot of the table. But like Henry, Ephraim was torn in two ways. If he let her go again without saying anything, when would he have another chance? Would he ever? What if she married someone else? The time while they were back here was painful, filled with anger and grief, and yet it would still slip by too quickly for him.

"Not quite a valley," Naomi answered, and her face too lit with the excitement of her inner vision. "I've heard of a geological phenomenon unlike any other in the world: a gorge so deep you can see almost the whole history of the earth in it." Her voice quickened. "The American Indians speak of it as a holy place, but then the whole earth is sacred to them. They treat it with a respect if we ever felt, we have forgotten. Perhaps we did anciently? Druid times? But this canyon is so beautiful it is beyond description, and bigger than anything we could imagine. I am going to see that, and climb down it to the river." She stopped and turned to Antonia. "I'm sorry. We're all getting carried away with our dreams. What are you going to do? You have a treasure as well, a whole new world to explore. What about Joshua and his music? Are we one day going to be a footnote in history as the family of the English Mozart?"

Antonia blushed, but it was with pleasure. "Perhaps," she answered, meeting the mood with hope and optimism of her own. "As soon as he is old enough we . . . I . . . shall send him to the musical academy in Liverpool. It will be terribly hard to part with him, but it is the only way he will get the education that is right for him. I can go and spend time there now and then, to be near him. It is the right thing to do." She looked to Henry for his agreement.

He realized how bitterly hard it was going to be for her to bring up such a remarkable child alone, make the decisions, try to be both mother and father to him.

And he was about to add an even greater burden for all of them, but he could not remain silent. He could feel Naomi's eyes on him also—waiting.

He cleared his throat. "I went to Kendal today," he began. He could feel his stomach tightening and in spite of the fire and the good food, he was cold.

They were waiting, knowing he would go on and tell them the reason.

"I went to see Percival, the forgery expert . . ."

"We all know it was forged," Ephraim interrupted him. "It's already been proved in court! We need to show that Judah was murdered, and that Gower did it, out of hatred and revenge."

"For heaven's sake, let him finish!" Benjamin said tartly. "Why did you go, Henry? What can Percival do to help?"

"I think it would be best if I gave you the whole story I found out," Henry answered. "Rather than follow my path of discovering that Mr. Percival dislikes Gower intensely, so much so that he seems to have allowed his animosity to govern some of his decisions. He admitted he was quick to come to conclusions, and to pass them on to Judah."

"Are you saying that he was wrong?" Ephraim demanded. "That is the only fact that matters."

Henry ignored his manner because he understood the emotions that drove it. "The date made the property legally Ashton Gower's, but the forgery was so bad it could never have passed for genuine."

"We know that," Benjamin agreed. "Ashton Gower is both a villain and a fool."

"No," Henry contradicted him. "He may have killed Judah, which would make him a villain, but he is not a fool. And if you think about it honestly, you know that." He leaned forward across the table. "Percival gave me the name of the original solicitor, who was not called to testify. He did not believe the deeds were forged, but he is not an expert. He was willing to be overruled."

"Your point, Henry?" Benjamin asked. "All this means nothing."

"Yes it does, Benjamin," Henry replied. "Overton read the deeds very carefully. He remembered the date in particular."

Naomi drew in her breath sharply.

"It was the same date as on the forged deeds," Henry told them.

"That's ridiculous!" Ephraim exploded. "Why in God's name forge something and make it exactly the same?"

"Because it was obviously a forgery," Henry answered. "And the original had been destroyed. Naturally, like you, everyone assumed that the original had been different."

They looked stunned. He turned to each of them, one by one. It was Benjamin who realized the meaning first.

"You mean the original gave the dates that make it Ashton Gower's?" he said incredulously.

"Yes."

"Oh, God! It . . ." he stopped.

Antonia was ashen. "Judah didn't know!" she said hoarsely. "He would never lie! Never!"

"Of course he didn't," Henry agreed instantly. "But he was, as you say, an honest man, not just outwardly, but of heart and mind deep through. He went back over all he had done to prove to Ashton Gower that he was wrong. And he found what I did. He saw Overton as well, and knew that the land was Gower's. That was the day he died."

"You mean the day he was murdered!" Ephraim almost choked on the words.

"Yes."

"What a hideous irony!" Ephraim was white-faced, his hands clenched into fists on the table. "Gower was right, and Judah could have told him, if Gower hadn't murdered him first. He could have had his name cleared . . ."

"Are we sure it was Gower who killed him?" Henry asked.

Benjamin stared back.

Ephraim sat rigid.

It was Antonia who spoke. "We are supposing it

was he because we also believed he forged the deeds. If he didn't, then perhaps he didn't kill Judah, either."

"Revenge," Ephraim said quickly. "If he was innocent, then he had a justified anger. Especially if he believed Judah forged the deeds so we could buy the estate."

"That's true," Henry agreed. "But if Judah was going to tell him the truth, then whoever did forge them, and certainly someone did, then that person had a great deal to lose. The case would be opened up again and . . ." Now he had to say it, although it twisted like a knife inside him. "And the estate given back to Gower. And if it proved to be Colgrave who forged it, and since it was in fact he who benefited from the sale, the law would look very seriously at him."

They all stared at him aghast.

"We bought it legally, at a fair price," Benjamin said quietly.

"I know that," Henry answered. "But you bought it from Colgrave, and it was not his to sell."

Ephraim looked around the table at each of them in turn. "That's monstrous!" he burst out. "Are you saying that if all this is true, then legally the estate, our home, belongs to Ashton Gower after all?"

"Is it true?" Antonia whispered.

Benjamin looked at Henry, hope struggling with knowledge in his eyes.

"Yes," Henry nodded.

Ephraim struggled to keep hope. "Unless Gower did kill Judah. If he did, then he can't profit from his crime. Apart from morally, that's the law. He'll be hanged."

"We didn't consider Peter Colgrave regarding Judah's death," Benjamin pointed out. "We were so morally sure that it was Gower. But this makes it different. It also explains why Judah would meet him at the lower crossing. It's only a few hundred yards from Colgrave's house. He might even have been there, and Colgrave followed him out." He turned to Henry. "Do you know what Judah was going to do about this?"

"Not from Overton," Henry replied. "But I knew Judah, just as you did. He was a man of honor. There is only one thing he could have done."

Again the silence was painful.

It was Naomi who spoke at last. "Give it back to Gower?"

"Isn't that what he would do?" Henry asked. "You knew him. Would he have kept that secret, and stayed living here, with Gower branded a forger, and left penniless?"

It was Antonia who answered. "No. No, he would never have done that. He couldn't."

"And he would not have let Colgrave go either," Benjamin added. "And Colgrave would have known that."

Ephraim looked from one to the other of them.

"Would he really have gone to Colgrave's house alone, at that hour of night, to face him with it?"

"No," Benjamin said with certainty.

"If he was going to give the estate back to Gower, with everything that means," Henry said slowly, "his first concern, after doing the right thing, would be to have made some provision for Antonia and Joshua."

"You can't buy a house at that time of night!" Benjamin said, with something close to derision in his face.

Henry bit his lip. "Benjamin, with the estate gone, there would be no money with which to buy a house," he pointed out. "And since it was a miscarriage of justice of very great proportions, there may have been an inquiry. Gower may not have let it rest in peace. He might have sued . . ."

Ephraim swore and buried his head in his hands.

"Then who?" Naomi asked. "Who could help?"

Henry turned to Antonia. "Whom did he trust? Who would be wise, discreet, and unfailingly kind?"

Her eyes were full of tears. "Apart from you? I don't know."

Henry found himself blushing at her trust, even after what he had been obliged to tell her. If she had hated him for it, at least for a while, he would not have blamed her. He wished he could offer something stronger or of more use than friendship.

"A friend?" Ephraim asked. "He would know we were all coming, but we don't live here. Who else?"

Benjamin rubbed his hand across his brow. "Actually, Ephraim, if we lose the estate, we may very well all live here. There'll be no income to support us anywhere else. In fact not even here, come to that. It'll change all our lives."

"Only if Gower is not guilty," Ephraim said, but now there was no hope in his eyes. It was as if within himself he knew, he was simply finding the strength to face it. All his passion and dreams were crumbling, towers that had shone in the air only an hour before. If ever he needed courage it was now.

No one bothered to argue with him.

"The Reverend Findheart," Antonia said, looking at Henry. "That must have been where he was going. It makes sense now."

"Then I will go and see him in the morning," Henry answered. "Unless you prefer to go?" he looked at Benjamin, then at Ephraim.

"No. Thank you." Benjamin looked bruised, as if the emotional shock had hurt him physically. "I had better look at the estate papers, and see what can be saved of ours. If there is anything. Ephraim, will you help?"

Ephraim nodded and reached out his hand to rest it on Benjamin's.

Henry rose to his feet and excused himself. They should be allowed time alone together. There was too much to face for it to be done easily, or quickly. He bade them good night, even though it could not possibly be so, and went upstairs to his room.

The morning was cold with flurries of snow. It was two days until Christmas. Henry had tea and toast alone in the dining room, then put on his greatcoat, hat, scarf and gloves, and set out to walk to the lower crossing of the stream, and the climb beyond.

He would have given anything he could think of not to be bound on this errand. The land was beautiful, great sweeping hills mantled in snow, black rocks making patterns through the white, steep sides plunging to the water. Wind-riven, the ragged skies were scattered with clouds and light, casting swift-moving shadows over the earth. Trees were stark, soft flakes blurring the edges even as he looked.

The estate itself had a wealth and a beauty it would tear the heart to leave behind. The Dreghorns had been good husbanders of its wealth. They would leave it far richer than Geoffrey Gower had. But Henry had no doubt for even a second, a passing instant, that this is what Judah had begun, and would have finished had not Colgrave killed him. He had a wrong to undo, whatever the cost. He would have made no excuse.

He reached the stream, swift-flowing under the flat stones that stretched across, like planks. He could never forget that this was where Judah had died.

He set out across the narrow way, taking small steps, balancing with his arms out a little. He did not care if he looked foolish.

The stone church with its squared tower was visible as soon as he rounded the corner of the hill, with the large vicarage beyond it, the orchard trees bare now, coated only with a dusting of snow. The lake water shimmered in gray and silver, always moving.

Henry trudged through the unbroken white, leaving his footprints to mark his way. At the gate he stopped, fumbling for the latch. It was indecently early to visit an elderly man. Perhaps he had been precipitate? He was still standing uncertainly when the front door opened and he saw the vicar regarding him with interest. He was thin and bent with white hair blowing in the gusts of wind.

"Good morning," Henry said, a trifle embarrassed at being caught staring.

"Good morning, sir," Findheart answered with a smile. "Would you like a cup of tea? Or even breakfast?"

Henry undid the gate latch and went in, closing it carefully behind him.

"Thank you," he accepted.

He was inside with his wet shoes and coat taken by an ancient housekeeper, and sitting by the fire in the dining room in his stocking feet with hot tea, toast, and honey, before he approached the subject for which he had come.

"Reverend Findheart, I was a close friend of Judah Dreghorn's . . ."

"I know," Findheart said mildly. "The night he was here, he spoke of you, just before he died."

Henry was grateful to be helped; it would be hard enough. "I went to Kendal and spoke to Mr. Overton. I know now what Judah learned. Is that what he said to you that evening?"

"Yes." Findheart added nothing, but he kept smiling, his blue eyes infinitely gentle. It was a confidence he was still not going to break. Henry would have to spell it out.

Henry sighed. "He learned that Ashton Gower was innocent, and the estate really did belong to him. Judah was going to give it back, wasn't he?"

"Yes. It was the only honorable thing to do," Findheart agreed. "Do have some more tea. You must be cold."

Henry accepted. "Did he ask you to care for Antonia, and her son, if he should be unable to?"

"He did. But of course that will only be necessary should they carry through Judah's wishes." He did not make it a question, but in effect, it was.

"Yes, they will," Henry said softly. "They are Dreghorns, too. But it will leave them all without means. Benjamin will have to give up his archaeology in the

Holy Land. Ephraim will not be able to go back to Africa, and Naomi too will have to remain here in England. I am not aware if Nathaniel left her with anything, but I imagine it would be only what income he had from the estate. And of course there are Antonia and Joshua. They will be without a home or means of any sort."

"I know," Findheart said. "I have given it much thought. The answer seems to me quite clear. I have served in this church for thirty years, and loved it dearly, but it is time for me to retire. I am getting old." He smiled ruefully. He must have been long past eighty. His eyes were bright but his skin was withered and his hands were veined in blue. "I have not the strength for the pastoral work that I used to have," he went on. "The people need and deserve a younger man, one better able to ride to the sick in the outlying farms and dales, one who can answer their call for the frightened, the sick and the lonely, the grieving and the troubled, at any hour. Benjamin Dreghorn is ordained to that office. He may take my place, and serve God here."

He lifted his hand in a small gesture. "The vicarage is large and warm, well suited for a family. There would be room for Antonia and Joshua, and for Ephraim, too, if he wishes, and for Naomi. It would shelter them all. There are vegetables in the garden and fruit in the orchard, if anyone will labor to make it yield." He smiled apologetically. "It is not the new and exciting botany of Africa, but it will feed the people, and to spare. And there is honey in the hives, and fish in the stream and in the lake."

Henry was grateful, and amazed at the simplicity of it. In a bolt of memory like a physical shock he heard again Naomi's words that the garden where Mary Magdalene recognized the risen Christ was not a physical place, but one of the mind, and of the spirit.

"Thank you," he said aloud. "I will tell them." He was unsure how to say to this gentle, generous-hearted man that they may find the loss too profound to be graceful about it for some time yet.

Findheart nodded. "Of course," he agreed. "Of course. But I shall make it all ready for them, at least for Antonia, if that is what she chooses. You are a good friend, Mr. Rathbone. Your presence will make it less difficult for them than it might have been. Judah Dreghorn was a man of the utmost integrity of heart. No other course is open to those who would be his heirs."

Henry found his throat suddenly constricted and his eyes prickled with tears. Sitting in this quiet vicarage with the fire burning gently in the hearth and the snow drifting pale flurries outside, he was more truly aware of how much he missed Judah, not just his company, his laughter, but the certainty of honor in him, that truth inside which was never tainted.

He sat for another half hour, learning more about

the church and the vicarage and what abundant room it offered for all of them. Then he thanked Findheart, put on his shoes, now nearly dry, and his coat, scarf, and gloves, and set out to retrace his steps, already vanished in the snow.

*I*t was nearly eleven in the morning by the time he was back in the house. Benjamin met him in the hallway. He looked tired, as if he had slept little.

"Yes," Henry said immediately. "Judah went to Findheart."

"What can Findheart do? He's the vicar of a village church, and must be closer to ninety than eighty." There was despair in Benjamin's voice, edging on bitterness.

Henry plunged in. He was aware of Antonia coming down the stairs with Joshua on her heels.

"Give you his living at the church," Henry replied simply. "You are ordained to the priesthood. You can serve God better here than unearthing the stones of the past in Jerusalem. Here you are needed. And the vicarage is large enough to accommodate you all, and with room to spare."

"All?" Benjamin was startled.

"There will be no means from the estate to provide

anything else," Henry pointed out. "There is no heritage for any of you, Benjamin, except the one nobody can spend or take from you, a name of honor above that of any other I know. Judah Dreghorn was a man of integrity like a star that cannot be dimmed. There was no shadow in him."

Antonia caught her breath and buried her face in her hands. Very slowly she sat down on the stairs, and Joshua put his arms around her.

Ephraim came out of the study doorway where apparently he had been listening. Naomi came from the other direction, looking at Henry, then at Ephraim.

"Of course," Benjamin said at last. "I'm sorry. I wasn't thinking. Yes, we will do very well there. Ephraim?"

It was too soon. Ephraim looked stunned, like a man who has seen darkness come at midday, and cannot believe it.

Naomi walked over to him, and slowly his eyes met hers.

He did not know what to do, he was so hurt.

Antonia lifted her face. "And I'm proud that he knew we would do the same thing," she said quietly. "He did not doubt us either, not any of us. And he was right. We will do what he would have. The land and the house and everything in it will go back to Ashton Gower, because it is his by all the moral laws. What we lose if we do this will be nothing compared with what we would lose if we did not. We would lose ourselves, and we would lose the love Judah would have felt for us, and the right to belong to him."

Ephraim looked at her with a sudden burning of pride, then at Naomi standing in front of him. "I can understand Gower," he said with difficulty. "He has suffered appallingly, and unjustly. He's a miserable swine, but perhaps in his place I'd have been no better."

Naomi smiled at him with a total and glowing warmth. "Probably worse," she agreed, but she said it so gently that he blushed with deep, almost painful joy.

The following day it was accomplished at law. They all took the train to Penrith, and with Ashton Gower present, swore to the events as they now knew them. Overton had been sent for from Kendal, and he also testified to his knowledge of Judah's discovery, and his intentions.

The police were advised of what seemed now inevitably to have been Colgrave's part in it. They instituted investigations that they had no doubt would lead to his arrest for both the forgery and the murder of Judah Dreghorn.

"A man of the utmost honor," the magistrate said of Judah, speaking with intense feeling. He looked at Joshua, who had asked to be with them. "You have a proud heritage, young man. You can look anyone in England in the eye, and bow your knee to no one, except the Queen."

"Yes, sir," Joshua answered quietly. "I knew that before."

"I imagine you did," the magistrate said with a nod. "At least you believed it. But it takes a bitter test of all that he has to make a hero like your father. Sometimes we bring to a struggle or a cause the gifts we see most clearly, a courage, a strength, or a charm others have told us we have. But often we find more is asked of us than that, more than we intended or thought we possessed. We are asked to offer that which we thought dearest, to forgive what seemed unpardonable, to face what we feared the most and endure it. Sometimes we have to travel to the last step a path that was not of our choosing. But I promise you this, young man, it will lead to a greater joy in the end. The difficulty is that the end is beyond our sight, it is a matter of faith, not of knowledge."

Joshua nodded, but he did not know what to say.

Antonia rested her hand on his shoulder. Her face was calm through her tears, but in her eyes was a fierce pride, and a certainty of understanding.

Ephraim put his arm around Naomi and she did not move away.

Benjamin offered his hand to Ashton Gower.

Slowly Gower reached across and clasped it. "He's right," he said with something like surprise, as if he were watching a light breaking across the horizon. "Judah Dreghorn was a man of the highest honor. I'll say that to anyone. You all are. I don't know that we'll ever be friends, there's too much hard history between us, and I've said and done ill by you. But by the Lord in Heaven, I admire you!" He turned and offered his hand to Ephraim.

Ephraim took it and held it hard, even with warmth. "I'm sorry," he said. "I spoke badly of you, and it was untrue."

Gower nodded. "Christmas tomorrow," he said. "Chance to start over. Do it better this time." And then he turned to Henry. "Thank you," he added simply.

ANNE PERRY is the bestselling author of the World War I novels *No Graves As Yet, Shoulder the Sky,* and *Angels in the Gloom;* as well as four holiday novels: *A Christmas Journey, A Christmas Visitor, A Christmas Guest,* and *A Christmas Secret.* She is also the creator of two acclaimed series set in Victorian England. Her William Monk novels include *Dark Assassin, The Shifting Tide,* and *Death of a Stranger.* The popular novels featuring Thomas and Charlotte Pitt include *Long Spoon Lane, Seven Dials,* and *Southampton Row.* Her short story "Heroes" won an Edgar Award. Anne Perry lives in Scotland. Visit her website at www.anneperry.net.